MOTIVATING
CHILDREN

Steering Children
In The Right Direction

Gordon Nosworthy

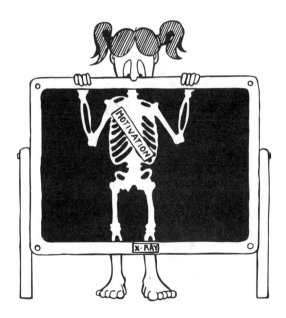

Published By

LEARNING PATH PUBLICATIONS
Box 273, Thornhill Ontario
L3T 3N3

Editor: Dr. Ian Anart

All rights reserved.
Published by Learning Path Publications
in cooperation with MMS, Toronto.

Copyright 1992 by Gordon Nosworthy
First Printing July/1992
Cover Illustration Tyler Serr
Cover Design Charlene Nosworthy
Book illustrations by Tyler Serr
Typesetting & Printing by Becker Associates
Printed in Canada
Editor: Dr. Ian Anart

ISBN 0-9695415-1-1

THANK YOU ALL VERY MUCH

Writing a book is never the work of one person. Recognizing every-one who helped me write MOTIVATING CHILDREN, or who influ-enced the content, would require more space than I have available. To all the people who at various stages read the manuscript, I cannot thank you enough. Your help really was appreciated.

I also want to thank the following people in particular. Your inter-est, expertise, and practical suggestions made the whole process a great deal easier. I did not always like what you said, but I did listen.

• Dr. Ian Anart, my major editor, for his assistance, advice, patience, and for the long nights we spent together exploring ideas;

• Karen Wood for her painstaking reading of a middle draft and for showing me how little things can make a big difference;

• Sharron Hart and Darlene Donovon who had the stamina to read all the way through the earliest draft and provide many encouraging ideas;

• Kay Kovack and Lynda Turner for reading a nearly completed edition and posing questions requiring productive rethinking;

• Charlene Nosworthy who read all the editions with a patience which was truly Olympian - a great deal of her is in this book;

• Luke Nosworthy and Ki Nosworthy for their help in editing the manu-script, and providing so much experimental data. Ki also provided the drawing of the car found in Chapter 19 and Luke also helped make many important decisions;

• Tyler Serr for supplying the wonderful illustrations which add so much to the text;

• Learning Path Publications for their confidence and support;

• To all the children and adults I have had the pleasure of working with, and learning from, over the years;

• Above all, I am massively indebted to the many writers and thinkers who have talked to me through their books and opened up so many wonderful doors.

---

*Come to the edge
He said
No, they said
We are afraid
Come to the edge
He said
They came
He pushed them
And they flew*

Guillaume Apollinaire

TABLE OF CONTENTS

A WORD TO PARENTS ONLY   Page   7

A WORD TO CHILDREN   Page 15

Chapter 1   We Can Fix Life When It Breaks   Page 19

Chapter 2   Born To Feel Special   Page 27

Chapter 3   Beliefs Are Invisible   Page 35

Chapter 4   Painting Your Walls Purple
Is Your Decision   Page 41

Chapter 5   Luck Is Not An Accident   Page 47

Chapter 6   Your Choices Are Who You Are   Page 53

Chapter 7   Feelings Are Difficult To Explain
In words   Page 61

Chapter 8   Smiling Really Is Logical   Page 67

Chapter 9   The Snake Goes Hiss The Dog Goes
Woof And The Computer Says
That Does Not Compute   Page 73

Chapter 10   What You Do Does
Make A Difference   Page 83

Chapter 11   The Glass Is Either Half Full
Or Half Empty   Page 89

Chapter 12   Rudolph The Red Nosed Reindeer
Learned How To Reframe   Page 95

Chapter 13   Life Is A Series Of Problems
Bound Together By Solutions   Page 101

Chapter 14   Your Refs Have Their Rules
And Blow Their Whistles
In Your Ears   Page 109

Chapter 15   We Are All Experts
In Constructing Walls   Page 117

Chapter 16   You Are Not A Prisoner
Of Your Frozen History   Page 121

Chapter 17   Anger Is Normal But
              That Doesn't Make It Right   Page 125

Chapter 18   You Kan't Lose Unless
              You Think You Kan   Page 131

Chapter 19   Your Automatic Pilot Works
              Without A Whole Lot
              Of Thinking   Page 135

Chapter 20   Failure Is Only A State Of Mind   Page 145

Chapter 21   Talk It Over With Yourself   Page 149

Chapter 22   Expecting The Worst Does Not
              Result In Getting The Best   Page 155

Chapter 23   Freedom Is Something
              You Learn   Page 161

Chapter 24   Love is the Ultimate I.Q. test   Page 165

FIND YOUR BELIEF QUOTIENT   Page 183

A WORD TO PARENTS ONLY:

This Book Is About Steering Your Child In The Right Direction

THIS BOOK IS ABOUT CHILDREN, BELIEFS & MOTIVATION

Why is it that one child will see peas as odious, little green balls, while another child will find them at least edible, perhaps even tasty?

Why is it that one child will give up immediately when confronted with a math problem, while another will view the same problem as a challenge?

Why is it that one child will be anxious and timid, while another will be confident and assured of a place in the world?

Why is it that one child will be responsible, while another walks around leaving a trail of uncapped jam jars, open drawers, crumpled towels, and unfinished business?

Some children are who they are because that is the way they came into the world. It is entirely possible that heredity can be responsible for some children being born confident, committed to tasks, even with a highly developed dislike for peas.

In the vast majority of cases, however, abilities aren't anchored in a child's personality at birth. Virtually all children enter the world with about the same degree of potential and the problem is not in having potential, but in learning how to use it.

Experience helps children develop beliefs, and beliefs in turn help children create the world they live in. When linked, beliefs form into a child's motivation engine by helping to decide what is wrong and what is right, what is moral and immoral, and generally how much effort to place into living.

What children think of the world is as important as the way the world really is, and because of this they have the power to accept responsibility for how they feel, what they think, and the things they do. The choice is a very real one for children, to embrace life or to avoid it, and parents can help develop the beliefs which motivate those fundamental decisions.

PARENTS ARE NOT BUTTERFLIES

Although it is never said out loud, people seem to share an unwritten assumption that something magical happens when a child comes onto the scene. This supposition holds that the birth of a child mysteriously trans- forms a man or a woman into a knowledgeable caregiver. No one under-

stands how it happens, or even exactly what makes it happen - it just seems to happen. The same biological mystery which turns a caterpillar into a butterfly is supposed to turn an adult into a parent.

Unfortunately, not many people get turned into butterflies when a baby is born, and there is far more hard work than magic in nurturing children. Parental wisdom does not mysteriously appear as a necessary part of the birth process. Not many parents suddenly become blindingly smarter when they are confronted by dirty diapers and a messy home. Few of us become professional counselors the first time our children come home crying and upset because of hurt feelings. The hormonal teenager continues to remain a mystery and there is no magic which allows us to suddenly gain an insight into their sudden mood shifts and swift mind changes.

Too often the magical view of parenting doesn't prepare people for all the learning which must take place. Instead of being filled with wisdom, most parents find that they become filled with awe with the arrival of their children, an awe which quickly turns to bewilderment as the children grow older and the full extent of their needs becomes apparent.

Just because the task of parenting is taken on willingly, doesn't make the job any simpler, or easier to understand. Parenting is hard work, and effective parenting is extremely hard work. Being committed to helping children is important, but knowing what to do is equally important, and that requires considerable planning.

RESPONSIBLE PARENTS

Sooner or later all responsible parents need to rise above the awe they feel to ask themselves what they can really do to help their children. What can we do to help our children think in ways which will bring success? Is there a way to help them feel happy and fulfilled? What steps can we take to prepare our children well enough so that they will know the difference between right and wrong when they encounter difficult situations like drugs or alcohol or violence?

It is really unfortunate that there are no hard and fast rules which parents can apply to their children which will result in reasonable behavior. It would be ideal to apply RULE #2 to a child with the certainty that it would turn that child into a law abiding citizen. Life doesn't work that way, and neither does parenting. That should make all of us breathe a sigh of relief because now we can see that all those parenting mistakes we have made are normal. Being the understanding caregiver can sometimes require more energy than even dedicated parents have at their disposal.

There is no such thing as the perfect child, the perfect method of parenting, or the perfect parent. Even responsible parents can expect the unexpected to happen. We may do all the things we are supposed to do, listen attentively, refuse to mini lecture, have family meetings, encourage rather than praise, and all the thousand and one other things a responsible parent is supposed to do, and find that it doesn't work because our children sometimes don't live on the same planet we do.

Of all the millions of species of life on earth, humans are the only ones capable of improving their lives to any serious and meaningful extent. This is accomplished as a result of the choices we make. Children do not always know the best choice to make. They are not always responsible for the urges and wishes which come to them, but they are responsible for the urges they act upon, and the thoughts which they choose to make a part of their lives.

The reason so many children are sad and dissatisfied is because happiness, success and personal meaning are hard to achieve and require especially difficult choices. Self-esteem is a birthright, but only if it is nurtured and grown in the right environment.

The wrong choices end up determining the quality of life just as much as do the right choices. The best thing parents can do for their children is to help them help themselves. By guiding children to an understanding of the vast potential they are born with, and by helping them develop the internal guidance necessary to tap into that potential, parents prepare their children to become all they can possibly be.

CHILDREN ARE NOT RANDOM CREATURES

Children are not random creatures. Although their actions may not be entirely predictable, they nevertheless fall into a given range.

A child, for example, doesn't just decide to act like a bully for no reason. The possibility of being a bully must first exist somewhere in the child, waiting to be acted out.

Children don't just abruptly decide they can't do math and that it is boring. A large number of possibilities must be in place before math becomes difficult to understand and difficult to study long enough to gain comprehension.

It takes a lot of work for children not to feel defeated simply because it seems that they are, but that possibility alone is probably more responsible for success and happiness than are intelligence and ability.

A child just doesn't suddenly decide that failure should be something to learn from rather than hide from. Believing in their own abilities is not something which surprisingly sprouts out of a child's mind without any previous information to allow the idea to exist or make it grow.

The possibility for self-fulfilment, and for all the other qualities which are necessary for a successful life, must first have solid roots before they can gain enough power to be actualized. If you want an apple tree, you must first plant an apple seed. If you want a successful child, you must first plant the seeds of success.

CHILDREN CAN'T BE WHAT THEY KNOW NOTHING ABOUT

Children can only be what they believe is possible. The beliefs they develop and store in their motivation systems provide them with information on how to feel, what to think, and what to do under certain situations. Each belief represents a system of possibilities which determines what can happen.

Beliefs are skills, in the same way that riding a bicycle and skating are skills. Just as parents deliberately teach their children how to cook or ride a bicycle, they can deliberately help them open up the possibilities for positive and constructive beliefs.

We cannot expect our children to be something they know nothing about. What we wish our children to know, we need to teach them specifically. By increasing their options we allow them to grow according to what they can do, rather than what they can't do. If we want our children to be positive and responsible, we need to teach them the possibilities for such attitudes.

MOTIVATING CHILDREN BUILDING BLOCKS

The purpose of this book is to motivate children in a way which will lead them to motivate themselves. For motivation to be effective it must be persistent, and in order to be self-perpetuating it must originate from the inside rather than the outside.

There are a number of basic beliefs which are so fundamental to an effective motivation engine that they can justifiably be called building blocks. MOTIVATING CHILDREN deals with 25 of those basic building blocks covering such topics as anger, feelings, work, luck, fear, helplessness, failure, smiling and love.

Because the chapters have been kept short and the writing style has been kept as simple, children shouldn't encounter a great deal of difficulty when reading the material themselves, and they should be encouraged to do so. This allows MOTIVATING CHILDREN to be used in a variety of ways.

A child can read to a parent. Both adult and child can read together. An adult can read to a child. The chapters can be used as a resource for some kind of discussion. What is important is that the child gains a sense that by thinking, feeling and acting in a specific ways they can obtain specific results. The sense of control which this gives cannot be minimized.

THE PAY OFF

It is a strange irony that while raising effective, self-motivated children is hard work at the beginning, it ends up being easier in the end. It is relatively easy to raise ineffective children because all we really need to do is to sit back and let nature take its course. Caring for ineffective children, however, is a lot more work in the long run because they are less independent, less responsible, more needing, and far more demanding.

For parents wishing a helpful guide, the MOTIVATING CHILDREN WORK-BOOK is available. This handbook has been designed so that children can further develop the beliefs presented in these pages through a series of exercises and games. For details see the inside back cover.

A FINAL WORD OF CAUTION

Being a responsible parent not only means helping the child grow, it also means knowing when to stop helping and when to step out of the way. If we tried hard enough, and wanted to badly enough, and pushed hard enough, we could probably turn our children into our own versions of perfect little beings. But if we did so, we would rob them of the unique individuality which makes them so special.

Hundreds of years ago, the poet-philosopher Kahlil Gibran came to much the same conclusion. He essentially asserted that our job as parents is not to make carbon copies of who we are, or ram our thinking down our children's throats so that they can be made to parrot our ideas. Our job as parents is to give them love, but not to chain them to our love. Since he said it first, I will leave the final caution to him.

ON CHILDREN

Your children are not your children. They are the sons and daughters of life's longing for itself. They come through you, but not from you. And though they are with you, yet they belong not to you.

You may give them your love but not your thoughts for they have their own thoughts. You may house their bodies but not their souls for their souls dwell in the house of tomorrow which you cannot visit, not even in your dreams.

You may strive to be like them, but seek not to make them like you for life goes not backward, nor tarries with yesterday. You are the bows from which your children as living arrows are sent forth.

Kahlil Gibran

A WORD TO CHILDREN:

This Book Is About Steering Yourself In The Right Direction

THIS BOOK IS ABOUT YOU

Question: If you had a bucket, and you threw ten black marbles into it, how many white marbles could you take out?

Answer: This really isn't a trick question. You couldn't take any white marbles out of the bucket because there are no white marbles in the bucket. You can't take anything out of a bucket which was not first put in. That is a basic law of the universe: you can only take out of buckets what you first put into them.

In some ways life is not much different than a bucket. You can only get out of life what you put into it. If you put mostly black marbles into your life, then you can only expect to take mostly black marbles out of life.

If you are able to understand this simple idea when you are young then you have latched onto a fantastic secret: you get from life almost exactly what you put into it; what goes in, comes out; what goes around, comes around.

If you stick a whole pile of negative actions into life, then you can't expect life to give you back much more than a whole pile of negative results. Although this may not sound like much of a secret, there are large numbers of people, old and young, who can't quite seem to figure it out.

Many people are really surprised that life seems so hard. They really shouldn't be. If you are riding a bike and you steer it into a brick wall you should not be surprised that things end up being hard for you. If you want to ride your bike in comfort, then you have to steer in a direction that gets you where you want to go without hitting brick walls.

Life is about choices. This isn't just adult talk, or school talk about rules. Life is about the choices you make, and the choices you allow other people to make for you.

When you are young, many of the your choices are made for you by your parents. This is one of the things parents do. They use their own experience to make decisions for you.

As you grow older you will be faced with the job of gradually making more and more choices on your own, according to your own rules, and according to the things you believe in. The more choices you make for yourself when you are young, the more effective your choices will be when you are older because you will have had a lot more practice.

Life happens to you all the time in ways which are completely unexpected and there isn't anything you can do to stop it. You have no control over an apple falling from a tree and hitting you on the head. You didn't see the apple coming so how could you act to stop it? Even when you know something is going to happen you often have no way to change things. If you like someone and they don't like you back there is no way you can force things to change.

But just because life happens to you in ways that you don't like doesn't mean that you should just sit around and let life do what it wants. If you see an apple falling on you, it is your choice whether you stand there and let it fall on you, or move out of the way. If you are steering your way through life it is your choice whether you continue in the same direction and collide with a wall, or turn in a new direction.

Fortunately for all of us much of life happens to us in ways that we expect. If we start out to go swimming on a hot summer afternoon, we usually get to go swimming. If we start out wanting to read a good book chances are excellent that we will find a good book to read. Maybe it won't be the first book we pick up, but if we pick up enough books we are bound to find a book we want. It is this kind of thing that gives us some control in our lives.

If you give this book you are reading now a chance, if you hear what it has to say with an open mind, then it can help you put the things into life which will help you get what you want out of life.

The ideas in this book are powerful, but only if you let them be powerful. Whether you are reading this to yourself or to a parent, or whether someone is reading it to you, you will get out of it exactly what you choose to put into it.

A parent, a friend, a teacher or a book can only help point out the right direction, because in the end you do the driving and you decide where you want to go. Even with life happening to you in ways you don't like, you are still the driver and you can decide how to deal with what is happening, and how to steer around what is happening.

This book is not only about your parents, it is also about you. If you use it properly it will help you decide where you want to go, and then it will help you get there.

A PLAN
FOR STEERING YOURSELF
IN THE RIGHT
DIRECTION

Chapter 1

WE CAN FIX LIFE WHEN IT BREAKS

Have you ever heard of John Henry Fabre? He was a French bug scientist who lived about a hundred and sixty years ago. He spent a great deal of his time trying to figure out what life was all about by trying to understand what made bugs tick.

One of the bugs Fabre studied was the Processionary Caterpillar. This caterpillar taught him a lot about how the things we do determine the quality of our lives.

Processionary caterpillars got their name from the way they behave. When one caterpillar meets another, one will go in front and the other will follow behind to form a short line. As other processionary caterpillars are encountered they also join in until eventually they form into a procession.

Fabre put a number of processionary caterpillars on the rim of a flowerpot. Head to tail, head to tail, they formed a complete circle around the rim.

What Fabre found was that once in motion they stayed in motion. After 24 hours the caterpillars were still going round and round. After 36 hours Fabre placed green pine needles, the favorite food of processionary caterpillars, in the middle of the pot. But the food didn't seem to interest them at all.

The caterpillars continued to go round and round for 40 hours, and then for 48 hours, and then 60 hours, and then 72 hours.

The caterpillars completely ignored the food. They paid no attention to what must have been a tremendous need for rest. They seemed totally unaware of their surroundings and about what was happening inside their bodies. They just kept going round and round, not stopping for sleep, not stopping for drink, not stopping for the things they needed in order to stay alive.

Fabre watched as the processionary caterpillars went round and round for seven full days until finally, one by one, they dropped dead of exhaustion and starvation.

The caterpillars didn't seem to realize that nothing was forcing them to follow the caterpillar in front. They didn't seem to realize that they could have stopped for a rest. They seemed to be totally unaware that they had any choices.

Unfortunately for processionary caterpillars, they are born to follow each other and it is only the rare processionary caterpillar which does not join in processions. They really don't seem to be built for choices. They are born to be what they are.

Human beings are much luckier than processionary caterpillars. We have the potential to be almost anything we want to be. You can improve the quality of your life while the processionary caterpillar can only do what it has to do. You don't have to follow others - instead you can choose to follow your own thoughts and ideas and dreams.

Suppose you had a bicycle and it broke. Most of us would have some idea how to fix it. You would probably use tools such as pliers, wrenches, hammers and screw drivers. With tools such as these, and with the knowledge of how to use them, you are prepared for most mechanical problems. Because you are prepared most problems of that kind can be fixed and they don't tend to worry you so much.

But how do you fix life when it threatens to break, or actually breaks? What do you do when you are sad, or feel as if no one likes you? Life is not mechanical, and when it breaks tools such as pliers and hammers will not be able to fix it. What we need to fix life is another kind of tool, and fortunately for us we all are born with a complete set.

Some Life Tools

• the ability to change
• the ability to think things out
• the ability to make choices
• the ability to change how we feel
• the ability to make decisions
• the ability to control fear
• the ability to solve problems
• the ability to think positive
• the ability to feel good about ourselves
• the ability to take a risk

Jim and Jake were identical twins. They lived with their parents in a small house in the suburbs.

Even though they looked alike they thought very differently and believed in very different things. Jim was always very positive, and Jake was always very negative.

To help the parents understand the twins better, the decision was made to give each boy the type of present which would offer a challenge toward the way they usually thought.

Jake the pessimist was given a room full of toys, and Jim the optimist was given a room full of horse manure.

Later that afternoon the parents went to Jake's room. All the presents had been unwrapped and all the toys had been piled into a corner. Jake sat in the middle of the room crying.

"Why are you crying?" Asked the parents.

Jake replied, "I'm crying because the toys will break one day, and when they do they won't be valuable any more."

The parents went to the Jim's room and opened the door. They found Jim knee deep in the manure, digging madly with a shovel, wearing a big grin on his face.

"Why are you smiling?" Asked the parents.

"With such a big pile of manure," Jim replied happily, "there must be a pony hidden in here somewhere."

Growing up can be difficult. Everybody does it, but that doesn't make it any easier. Each of us is born, gets older, and learns some way of living in the world. Each one of us takes the tools we are born with and shapes them into a <u>motivational engine</u> which we carry with us for the rest of our lives. This engine helps us steer a path through life by helping us decide right from wrong, worthy from unworthy.

Hopefully, our motivational engine will help us feel successful, but there is no guarantee. There is no guarantee that success will come our way, or that we will be happy, in fact there is no guarantee to anything in life. The only guarantee is that life will basically turn out according to how good we are at fixing life when something goes wrong or when it breaks.

The motivational engine outlined below as an example is almost doomed to make the person holding it feel bad. Each of the beliefs works to make Tamara's social life more difficult. When combined these beliefs act to keep life at a distance rather than to invite life in with open arms.

Tamara's Motivational Engine

- no one likes me so I won't like them
- I am smarter than you
- I work hard and I am always right
- I can't dance but I can do math
- money is better than friendship

Life does not have to turn out for the best for us. Like Jake in the story above we can find unhappiness even in the middle of plenty. Or like Jim, we can find something positive and optimistic even in the midst of the worst smelling situations.

By feeling as if he has to cry, even in the middle of a pile of presents, Jake has not used his life tools as effectively as his brother. His life has something broken in it just as surely as a bike with a bent wheel is broken. Jake is a lot like the processionary caterpillar going round and round in the same circle while ignoring all the good things which pass by.

You are born with the ability to choose what will motivate you, what will excite you through life, what will move you to dream and hope. As you grow older the power to choose your motivation stays with you, it doesn't fade, it remains under your control. Only when you choose not to exercise that power will it disappear. But the moment you wish to take the power back again, it will return, immediately. That is the real power you are born with.

Our motivational engine acts just like a rocket's internal guidance system by steering us through life in the same way that an internal guidance system steers a rocket through space. If a rocket's guidance system doesn't work, then the rocket will not be very accurate. If our motivational engine doesn't work very well, we don't work very well either.

A rocket travelling the 389,157 kilometers to the moon will only be successful if its internal guidance system continually asks, 'Where am I?' and compares it to, 'Where am I supposed to be?' and then makes course corrections accordingly.

Our motivational engine helps us through life in just the same way. That is what motivation is all about. It helps us aim through life. It helps us make corrections on our journey by deciding which steps we need to take, and how we should go about taking those steps.

There are five to ten million different species of life on this planet: mice, flies, fleas, eagles, monkeys, processionary caterpillars, etc.. Of all those species, humans are the only ones capable of improving their lives to any

significant extent. Only humans can say, "I should really do this, but I really want to do that, so I will do that, and I will ignore the consequences of not doing this'.

Only humans can say, "I think I'll paint the walls purple and put in some red stripes." This gives humans a tremendous advantage over other animals. But it is not always something we all take advantage of. Too many of us pretend that we have no power over our motivation because if we did have that control it would mean we would have to work too hard to keep it up.

Motivation is about choices, and about the desire which allows you to make those choices. There really aren't many 'musts' or 'have tos' in life. Most of the things that we feel we must do are really things that we want to do, or decide to do, or feel we should do.

Conformity is deciding to choose what others are choosing without really having good reasons for the decisions. Conformity is going round and round the rim of a flower pot just because we are following the backside of someone in front of us. There is no real reason that we 'must' conform. Conforming can often make life easier for us, but that doesn't mean that it makes life better.

If you allow others to make your choices, then you won't have much to say about how your life unfolds. The sense of helplessness and frustration this produces can be very painful.

> *A farmer placed his young son on a donkey and started off for town. They passed some old men who saw the boy riding and grumbled, "Why is that healthy young boy riding while his poor father is walking?*
>
> *Things should not be done that way."*
>
> *Embarrassed, the farmer took his son off the donkey and let him walk while he rode instead.*
>
> *They passed some women who said, "A grown man riding while his son walks. Things shouldn't be done that way."*
>
> *Embarrassed again, the man pulled his son up onto the donkey and they both rode on.*
>
> *They passed some children who felt sorry for the donkey and said, "Imagine two healthy people riding on the back of*

*a small donkey. That isn't fair. That's not the right way to do
things."*

*The farmer and his son got off the donkey and together
they lifted the animal and carried him toward town.*

*While they were going over a bridge, the son tripped, this
threw the farmer off balance, and all three of them fell into
the water.*

The moral is simple: No matter how hard you try you can't please
everybody, but if you make choices based upon what you think is right you
can please yourself.

One of the great oddities of life is that the more effort you put into getting
better at something, the easier it eventually gets to do what you are doing.
That is exactly how motivation works.

It takes a lot more work to deliberately choose what is going to motivate
you. But once you do choose, the strength of your motivation helps you
overcome even more difficult problems requiring even more difficult
decisions.

It takes a lot of work to make plans and follow them through. But once
you achieve your goals, you feel a tremendous sense of satisfaction.

It takes a lot of work to keep yourself going when you don't really feel
like putting out the effort.

It takes a lot of work not to feel defeated simply because it seems that
you are.

After a while you get better at using your life tools and making your own
plans. And because the results make you feel better about yourself, you will
have the desire to make even more plans. You get stronger.

A lot of research has shown that the thoughts currently dominant in your
mind are really a reflection of your motivational engine. This means that if
we want to change our motivational engine all we have to do is change our
thoughts. Instead of thinking defeat, we can think success. Instead of
thinking of problems, we can think of solutions.

You can learn to use the tools you are born with. That is your birthright.
You can decide what your motivational engine is going to look like and how
it is going to operate. You are not responsible for all the urges and wishes
that come to you, but you are responsible for the urges you act upon and the
thoughts you choose to make a part of your life.

Chapter 2

BORN TO FEEL SPECIAL

Have you ever stopped to think about what it might feel like to be born? One minute you are warm, comfortable, cosy, just hanging around inside your mother, and then all of a sudden everything starts happening and the world starts spinning. You are pushed, pulled, twisted, squeezed, and forced through a space much smaller than you are.

You are painfully ejected into a glaringly bright light. For the first time ever in your life you feel cold air against your tender skin, and you hear sharp noises, and you feel rough hands grabbing you.

With all this happening to us why do almost all of us choose to keep on living? We all have the power to end our lives whenever we wish, so there must be some driving force inside us which gives us the strength to stay born. There have been a lot of explanations offered to explain why we don't just give up.

1. It has been said that people choose to live because they have a motivation to seek power. Somehow, the need to be important, or to boss people around, or to be respected, is enough to keep us alive and breathing.

2. It has been said that humans choose to live because without having to be told they understand the importance of greed and accumulation. The theory goes that humans are born with the need to accumulate large quantities of wealth, big houses and big cars, and a lot of expensive toys. Somehow this need is powerful enough to keep us wanting life to continue day after day.

3. It has been said that people choose to live because something in their bodies or their minds tells them that they should become the best they can possibly be.

4. It has been said that what motivates us is a need to survive, to keep on living. This would mean that being safe and keeping ourselves safe would be really important to us, and of course they are, so this theory has some chance of being true.

When you think about everything that happens during your birth, all the pulling and twisting and squeezing that goes on, none of these explanations are totally able to stand alone. They all need something more to complete them. None of them seem big enough, or important enough, to act as the basic motivation for life. Somehow they are not noble enough.

I seriously doubt that the first thing to pop into a baby's mind while being born is the need to be the general of an army, or a dentist, or an accountant.

I don't think that babies are born thinking that they better get started if they want to own a bigger house than their neighbors, or drive a more luxurious car. I don't think a child is born thinking it is a good idea to get busy and prepare to meet death.

The desire for wealth and power are things that babies learn from their families as they grow up. Someone has to tell babies that these things are important enough that they should spend their entire creative lives worrying about them and trying to acquire them.

Babies do seem to be born with the need to survive and stay safe. But keeping yourself safe is really only important if you feel special. Without

feeling special the fright and confusion of birth might make the whole business of surviving just seem like a lot more trouble than it's worth. A baby would need to feel more special than the pain and the confusion of being born, or the struggle to stay alive just might not seem worthwhile.

It is this feeling, this feeling of being important, of being significant and meaningful which makes us feel special enough to withstand the pain of birth. We are born feeling that we are the most wonderful and fantastic things in the universe. What we call motivation is really the method of problem solving we use to keep us feeling special.

After all, when you think about it, isn't the act of holding power just another way of saying that you are more special than those you have power over?

Isn't the act of being wealthy just another way of saying that you are more special than others who do not have as much wealth?

Even though we are all born feeling special, we do not all go through life feeling the same way. Far too many children learn from life that they are not special. Far too many children come to learn that they are wrong, that they are not likeable, that they are not worthy.

A person who feels special lives in a different world than someone who does not feel special. Life looks different, feels different, and tastes different.

When you feel special you like who you are. You feel as if you count, as if you have a natural right to dignity and respect. That is really important because most people try their best to avoid other people they don't like. When the person you are trying to avoid is your own self you get caught in a really painful, hurtful trap.

You really can't hide from your own self but you can pretend that you are hiding, and this can cause all kinds of problems. You are capable of doing all kinds of strange things to pretend you are hiding. You might turn into a very difficult person to get along with; or you might try to hide behind the things you own; or you might just simply hide by going peculiar in the head.

I once asked a number of grade 7 and 8 students a series of questions to find out some of the things they believed were important and valuable in life. One of the questions asked the students to rate the value of a Porsche on a scale of 0 to 10. Most of the students rated the expensive sports car as very valuable. That was expected.

The students were also asked to use an identical scale to rate their own value. Because the answers were kept secret and names weren't used, there is good reason to believe their responses were basically truthful. And because of that, the results were really surprising.

If those students felt valuable and special, most of them should have rated themselves at least as highly as the expensive Porsche. Sadly, over 90% of the students rated themselves less valuable than the car. They gave themselves less importance than an object made with human hands. They gave themselves less value than an object which only has value because people give it value.

Not feeling special is sad because our feeling of being special directs everything we do in life. To someone who feels special this world is full of opportunities, full of possibilities, full of choices. When you feel special you feel confident, you feel capable, you feel as if you have some control over what happens to you.

But when you don't feel special, when you feel all wrong, you make life seem much harder than it has to be. If you don't feel special then you have to work harder to prove your own worth. You always have something to prove. The differences between right and wrong aren't really important to someone who needs to prove his or her own worth no matter what it takes.

Many people who don't feel special will do almost anything to feel right, and many of the methods they choose cause themselves more harm than good.

If you feel bad, or wrong, or if you hurt inside, one of the easiest ways to make things seem okay is to lie to yourself. You might tell yourself that it's all right to steal because, after all, it's you who are doing the stealing, and you really have to find some way to ease the pain, and stealing seems to be easy.

But does stealing make you feel better? On the contrary, it usually makes you feel worse. The world around us tells us that stealing is bad, and when we do it, even though we feel we need to do it, we feel shame and guilt.

You might prove how special you are by eating and constantly trying to fill a hole in your self-image. Or you might try to feel special by being a bully, or by doing things that give you more rights than other people. You might even try to feel special by talking all the time and covering up your lack of self-esteem with a lot of empty words.

Feeling bad can become the only way of life that you know. You can actually get to the point where you begin to feel right about feeling wrong. You won't even be able to recognize something nice when it happens to you because you will be expecting only bad things to happen. Feeling wrong becomes natural. Being depressed or being nasty to other people and to your own self becomes the world that you live in. It becomes the way things are. At this point you don't know how to accept good things even when the opportunity arises.

Research is now beginning to prove what grandmothers have been saying for centuries: how you feel has a lot to do with your state of health. When you feel wrong, you just don't feel wrong in your feelings, you feel wrong with your whole mind and your whole body. If you feel sick in your head or heart long enough you will eventually find that you become sick in your body as well.

The first thing you need to ask yourself is, "How special do I feel?" If you find that you don't really feel so special then you need to stop and ask yourself why, and then you need to figure out a way to feel special again.

HOW SPECIAL DO YOU FEEL?

1. Y N Do I often doubt myself?
2. Y N Do I think other people are more right than I am?
3. Y N Do I like the person I see in the mirror?
4. Y N Do I do things to please others, even if the things
        I do aren't particularly important to me?
5. Y N Do I have goals which are my own?
6. Y N Do I know how to please myself?
7. Y N Am I happy more often than I am sad?
8. Y N Do I know what I want in life?
9. Y N Do I like other people?
10. Y N Do I think other people are better than I am?
11. Y N Am I afraid to speak my mind?
12. Y N Do I stand up for the things I believe in?
13. Y N Do I have firm beliefs?
14. Y N Am I proud of who I am?
15. Y N Do I know my accomplishments?
16. Y N Does the fear of failure stop me from taking risks?
17. Y N Can I forgive people easily?
18. Y N Am I jealous of other people?
19. Y N Do I want to be somebody else?
20. Y N Do I like who I am?

You were born to feel special, to feel dignity. If you didn't answer yes to most of the above questions, then there is a good chance you don't value either yourself or the things you stand for enough.

If this is the case it is up to you to figure out how to feel special again. No one else can do it for you. No one else can make you appreciate yourself. No one else can force you to give yourself credit for being special. No one else can make you appreciate your own value. When you do, you will learn that feeling special is its own reward.

A PLAN
FOR STEERING YOURSELF
IN THE RIGHT
DIRECTION

Chapter 3

BELIEFS ARE INVISIBLE

I once knew a woman who was afraid to leave her house. She imagined that if she left the safety of her home something bad would happen. She wasn't sure what this bad thing was, but she was certain that it would happen. The lawn might rise up to eat her, or the side walk might crack open and let a monster loose.

The fact that other people could come and go without getting eaten by the lawn did not seem to bother her at all. She believed that she would be harmed if she left the house, and that was that. That was her theory, and it became her world.

Many of us might sit back and think that we are somehow better than that woman. We might think that she was being silly. After all, we all know that lawns don't eat people.

Somehow, it is always easier to see the faults of others than it is to see our own. If we think we are better than that woman, we should not. There is a little of that woman in all of us, young and old alike. All of us have opinions which are just as silly and as harmful to us as that woman's belief was to her.

It is absolutely amazing what the human mind will accept as true just because we want it to be true. We don't really need proof of any kind. All we really need to do to believe is want it to be so.

What makes our belief system even more amazing is that we generally do not realize that we have any control over what we choose to believe. Somehow people won't admit how much control they have over their values and assumptions and expectations. It seems that we would much rather just pretend that we have no control at all, almost as if we want to be at the mercy of our convictions.

WE BELIEVE WHAT WE WANT TO BELIEVE

- life stinks
- life is absolutely great
- it is not important to have an opinion
- they are stupid
- they are very intelligent
- people who don't seem very bright can not change and become brighter
- intelligent life from outer space has visited earth
- there is no intelligent life in space
- there is no intelligent life on earth
- I can not carry a tune
- I can not sing
- I can not dance
- I can not speak in front of other people

Our lives are ruled by our beliefs. If we think we can not dance, we will probably never try to dance long enough or hard enough to prove to ourselves that everyone can learn how to dance at least a little bit.

Because we do not try to dance we will always assume that we cannot dance. Every time we come across dancing in our lives we will either dance poorly, or not try to dance at all, and we will prove to ourselves that we were right to hold that belief.

If we really wanted to learn how to dance, then we could learn how to dance. We may never be professional dancers, but there is nothing to prevent any of us from learning how to dance in some fashion because there are millions of ways to dance.

If that woman we were talking about earlier really wanted to leave her house she could. The grass really does not bite. She knows that. But she chooses to forget that she knows. There is no force in the world which says that she has to believe that the grass bites. She has chosen that idea. She can also choose the opposite idea if she wants.

If we do not think we can speak in front of other people chances are that we will never speak in front of other people long enough to prove that our belief was wrong. We will never give ourselves the chance of getting better by actually speaking in front of other people. As a result, each time we do not speak in front of other people, we will gather more facts to prove that we were right to hold that belief.

The convictions we hold are not visible. Because of this we seem to pick up our beliefs without realizing what we are doing. We don't realize that the ideas we select will control our actions and determine the kind of lives we will have. Because our convictions are invisible, we tend to forget what we are even carrying around inside of us.

For instance, some people do not like peas. They probably do not remember the exact moment when they decided that they did not like peas, but that does not prevent them from refusing to eat peas. They don't spend much time thinking about it, but when they do, they realize that they do not like peas. Not liking peas has become a part of them. This has become a belief, and it steers them through their meals.

Knowing that our beliefs steer us gives us the opportunity to take more charge of our actions. Knowing that we must somehow want something to be true in order for it to be true is a powerful tool.

You can do most anything you want to do that is possible to do if you believe you can. You can't jump off a cliff and fly. That is not human. You would fall like a stone and hurt yourself when you landed. But you can learn how to dance. You can learn how to sing. You can learn how to like who you are. You can learn to believe in yourself.

We do have control over the kind of world we live in. You don't have to stay confined to your house for the rest of your life, afraid to open windows, afraid to look out into the real world, afraid that the grass will bite you.

You can build a system of ideas which will open the doors and throw back the drapes and allow you to breathe in the fresh air.

You can if you believe you can, and unfortunately it is also true that you can't if you believe you can't.

A PLAN
FOR STEERING YOURSELF
IN THE RIGHT
DIRECTION

Chapter 4

PAINTING YOUR WALLS PURPLE IS YOUR DECISION

Intelligence is difficult to understand. We have all taken intelligence tests. The score we receive at the end of these tests is supposed to tell us something. Usually it is meant to tell us how well we can learn in school. This in turn is supposed to tell us how successful we will be in life.

These tests might seem important at first, at least until we discover that many many people who are successful in life, or who are happy in life, did not score well on intelligence tests and did not do all that well in school.

Intelligence seems to be more than just an ability to learn school stuff. I really don't know what 'intelligence' is, but much of what I do know about it I learned from watching a man I'll call Richard try to order a hamburger.

Richard came into a fast food restaurant while I was trying to eat and digest a burger and fries. Usually it isn't polite manners to stare at people, but I couldn't help myself. There was something about him which just kept me looking. I couldn't take my eyes off him.

Richard was tall and thin. He moved with short, jerky movements, but somehow his movements never seemed to finish what they started out to do.

For example, if Richard started to put his hand in his pocket it would not quite get there, but would stop instead just before it reached the pocket, and sort of hover there like a helicopter. He seemed somehow incomplete, like a circle that was not quite finished, or a drawing that was only a first draft.

He came into the restaurant with his son and his son's wife and family, meaning that there were three generations of Richards present and sitting almost beside me.

I watched Richard as he moved nervously up to read the menu on the wall. He looked, stopped, started back to his table, stopped, came back to look again, and then moved back to his family. When his son asked him what he wanted, Richard said he didn't know. And then he asked his son to choose for him.

Richard's son took the order from the rest of the family and started off toward the counter. Richard suddenly left his seat after his son and stopped him. Richard had changed his mind.

Richard looked at the menu again. He asked his son if he thought the restaurant served pizza. There was absolutely no indication on the menu that pizza was being served. His son said he didn't think so. Richard said he didn't think so either.

Richard asked his son what he was having. His son told him. Richard started back to his table and his son called after him to ask what he wanted to eat. Richard replied by asking his son if he was sure the pizza wasn't on the menu. The son said that if pizza was on the menu, did he want pizza? Richard said he didn't know.

The son returned to the table and I noticed that he walked a great deal like his father. His steps were also short and choppy. I realized then that both their steps were short and choppy because short steps allowed both of them the opportunity of changing their minds on short notice. If their steps had been long it would have committed them to longer term decisions.

Richard's son once again took the order from his family and started back to the counter. Richard stopped his son almost at the counter and added an order of french fries.

Richard's son turned around and went back to the table to ask how many wanted french fries.

Before Richard's son had made it back to the counter, Richard had again left his seat and walked quickly to his son and asked whether the restaurant sold chicken wings.

At this point the son began to lose patience and his face got a little flushed. The son asked Richard if he saw chicken wings on the menu, and Richard said no, and the son said that in that case they didn't sell chicken wings. Richard looked slightly surprised.

It was about this time that Richard's son's wife decided to take charge. She joined the two men and sharply told them both to sit down while she stood in line and ordered for everyone.

While she waited to be served I watched Richard's face as all the possible decisions he could have made crossed his mind and all the doubts which could have been made followed right behind.

What was sad about the whole funny affair was the youngest generation of Richards who were sitting quietly in their seats and watching the older generation of Richards deal with their problems, and learning.

I was watching because I had trouble believing what I was seeing, but they were watching because they were believing what they were seeing. Those children were developing a model of how to order a hamburger which would probably stay with them all their lives, just as Richard's son had also learned a model of ordering hamburgers from his father.

Intelligence is an ability which most humans are born with. Watching Richard taught me that the more intelligent a person is the more effective that person's decisions should be.

A plant doesn't seem to have a great deal of intelligence. The number of decisions a plant can make are seriously limited. Most of the things it does are automatic, and can't really be called decisions at all.

A human, on the other hand, seems to be able to make an infinite number of decisions. It is that decision making ability which lifts humanity out of the ranks of animals, insects, and processionary caterpillars and sets them up as beings who can make a difference in the universe.

Making a choice between alternatives is a sign that intelligence is directing that choice. But when we want to determine just how much intelligence is being used to make a decision, we need to look at something else. We need to look at the results of the choices we make and how effective they make us.

When a person is effective the things they do tend to work really well, and when they are ineffective the things they do tend to make things worse.

If you know you are hungry, but you can't make up your mind whether you want chicken legs or pizza in a restaurant which specializes in hamburger combinations, how effective does that make you?

If you know you hurt your friend's feelings but you deliberately choose not to try and make your friend feel better, just how intelligent are you? How effective are you?

The point that I am trying to make is that real intelligence is directly tied to the decisions we make in our lives. No matter how much potential intelligence poor Richard was born with the way he used his abilities made him less intelligent.

For all we know, Richard could have a very high I.Q. as measured on an intelligence test, but the truth is he was barely effective enough to order a hamburger in a hamburger joint.

Your decisions are who you are, and your decisions are made according to the beliefs you carry. The way we make decisions tells us a lot about who we are, the kind of people we are, and the kind of things that motivate us.

Your decisions tell the entire story of what goes on inside your brain and the beliefs that make you work. That is where real intelligence rests and not in some fantasy land where real problems don't exist. Without his daughter-in-law poor Richard would probably still be shuffling back and forth between one decision or another and he and his family would be really hungry by now.

Understanding the importance of making decisions is something that Richard should have learned when he was young. If he had learned the significance of making choices his life would probably have turned out much differently. If nothing else, it would have helped make his eating habits a lot easier.

A PLAN
FOR STEERING YOURSELF
IN THE RIGHT
DIRECTION

Chapter 5

LUCK IS NOT AN ACCIDENT

Human beings are very often far too clever for their own good. We think we know so much, even when we know so little - or maybe it is because we know so little that we think we know so much.

I once knew a teenager who wanted more than anything else to live on Easy Street. I don't know exactly where Easy Street is, what country or what city it is in, but I do know that a lot of people really want to live there. It is a very popular place.

The teenager's name was Jacob. He didn't know where Easy Street was, all he knew was that he wanted to live there. Jacob had quit school and was working part time as a caretaker while he worked like a fanatic on his dream.

Jacob played the lotteries. He showed me books in which he had neatly calculated his wins and losses for the previous years. He showed me the pages of statistics he used to work out which numbers were going to come up, in what order, and on what nights.

But Jacob never won.

Jacob had pages and pages of numbers which he believed had some meaning. He had a large number of systems which he had once believed would work, and had tried, but which did not work. He was constantly writing in his books and working and re-working the numbers and the methods he had in hopes that the magic method of winning would one day appear.

But Jacob never won.

Jacob showed an amazing amount of determination and persistence. Although he had some small successes, he lost almost all the time, and yet he found the stamina to continue. He wanted to win so that he would never have to work again, so that he could buy a mansion on Easy Street and drive a fancy car down tree lined avenues and live a life of luxury. He believed that his methods would one day work. He really believed they would.

I learned a lot from Jacob. He seemed to understand that you can't win if you don't play the game. But he did not seem to understand that if you spend your time looking for water in the middle of a desert, no matter how much work you put into your search, you are essentially doomed to failure before you even begin. Just looking for water isn't good enough. You also need to look for water in the right places.

Jacob chose to gamble. He knew the risks, but he also believed that luck was something that he could manipulate through some kind of magic. The odds against winning a lottery are fantastic. He knew that. Yet he also felt sure that luck would come to him.

Good luck charms, or whispering magic words to a midnight moon in the middle of a graveyard will not have any influence on luck at all. What Jacob really wanted was success. He wanted to obtain rewards. But he wanted to do it the easy way. He didn't seem to realize that he was trying to achieve luck the hard way, without earning it, which is really the most difficult way.

Jacob could have earned some luck. He could have stayed in school, for instance. School doesn't work magic but it does make things that might seem like luck happen more frequently.

He could have set a goal, made a plan, and then he could have made a whole pile of choices which would help him achieve that goal.

I know this sounds like familiar advice, but that doesn't make it any less important. Luck is not going to come begging you to let it in. Even selling vacuum cleaners door to door would have given Jacob more opportunity for success than picking a few numbers and sitting back to wait for the magic to happen.

Had Jacob placed all his hard work into smart work he might even be living on Easy Street by now. Instead, he is probably still making long lists of numbers and hoping beyond hope for something which he probably does not truly believe will ever really happen to him.

The people most of us consider the luckiest people are almost always the same people who work the hardest and the smartest. They are not successful simply because luck decided to smile upon them. That does happen, but not as often as you might think. They are successful and lucky because they deliberately removed as much of the element of chance as they could from the process of obtaining the goals they desired. All we see is their success, and we don't get a chance to see all the hard work which went into making that success possible.

Championship boxers don't become championship boxers just because they happened to climb into a ring one day and beat out the existing world's champion with a lucky punch. A championship boxer became a champion because he worked hard and worked smart and earned every bit of his luck. If luck had anything to do with championship boxing then we would see a lot of 90 pound weaklings wearing boxing crowns.

A medalist in a track and field event didn't become a medalist by a lucky run or a lucky jump or a lucky throw. A medalist became a medalist by working hard and working smart and earning luck.

Success in almost any field is not a result of blind luck. Blind luck does come to a few, but the few are so few that there aren't enough of them around to start a trend. Some people do strike it rich, and some people find themselves owning oil wells without any effort. Some people do find that they have been born with silver spoons in their mouths, but it takes more than luck to keep what you were given freely with birth.

Success comes to those who bring success with them, those who feel successful inside. And luck follows the same pattern.

Luck comes to those who make their own luck and carry it with them into life. Those people who expect life to hand them luck without any smart effort can virtually be assured of failure and disappointment.

A PLAN FOR STEERING YOURSELF IN THE RIGHT DIRECTION

Chapter 6

YOUR CHOICES ARE WHO YOU ARE

Have you ever wanted to know more about who you are? Have you ever wondered what you look like from the inside, or from behind? Have you ever wondered how other people see you?

When we take really close looks at ourselves we find that there is a lot more to who we really are than meets the eye. The person you see in the mirror when you brush your teeth and comb your hair is a very complex mixture of good and bad, success and failure, ambition and fear.

You are an incredibly complex, living thing. You are the same as everyone else in the world, and yet you are entirely and completely different. Because of this complexity, you are a mystery to people around you, and more importantly, even to yourself.

Not knowing who we are can cause problems of self-confidence and control. It can make it difficult to make plans, or know what is best for us. It is only when you have a good idea about who you are that you are able to decide on what beliefs you want to change, and which ones you want to be part of your motivational engine. This is the basis of free will.

There are many really complex ways of finding out more about who you are. Some of them involve years of study and years of analyzing yourself. Some of them cost a lot of money and need the help of very well paid experts. None of them are guaranteed to work.

Fortunately, there is a way of drawing a picture of who you are which is quick, accurate, easy, and doesn't cost any money. The only expert you need to do this method is yourself and it is guaranteed to work.

We are what we believe. What we believe is who we are, and what we are. The beliefs we carry in our minds are responsible for the choices we make. The choices we made in the past have made us who we are today. The choices we make today turn into who we will be tomorrow.

If you believe green ice cream gives you pimples, then it is highly unlikely that you will choose to eat green ice cream. On the other hand, if you want pimples you might choose green ice cream deliberately. The things we believe and the motivation they generate determines the choices we make.

In order to study our choices we need to examine the things we like, the things we don't like, the dreams we have, the worries we have, the hopes we have, how much self-confidence we have, how much we value ourselves, and how well we are able to love.

When you add all these choices up, the final sum you arrive at is your belief system, you arrive at who you are. By studying your choices you manage to make your beliefs visible.

The following choices will give you some idea of what you believe in. These are only a few of the choices open to you. There are millions more.

<u>YOU ARE YOUR CHOICES</u>

Why did you decide to comb your hair the way you presently comb your
 hair

Do you put things off until just before they are due

Are you late or early for appointments

Do you spend your time with a lot of different people or just a few people

Do you expect other people to entertain you

What kinds of things make you happy

What kinds of things make you sad

Do you complain a lot

Do you speak your mind

Do you let things bother you without speaking your mind

How do you act when you don't get your own way in an argument

Do you have a lot of feelings which you find difficult to control

Do you feel prejudice against other races or religions

What hobbies or pastimes do you have

Do you believe you are a success or a failure

Have you ever cheated on an exam

Do you think school is important

Are you able to use thinking to control your feelings

Do you act first and then think about what you did second

Are you able to stay calm in a crisis

Do you have a lot of opinions

Are your opinions well thought out

Do you like junk food

Do you give to charity because you think it is the right thing to do

Do you give to charity because everyone else is giving

Are you well organized

What kinds of things upset you

Do you like the answers you are giving to these choice questions

Are you being honest in your answers or are you trying to fool yourself

Do you trust other people

Do you believe what other people tell you

Do you swear

Do you feel embarrassed when you make a mistake

Do you argue a lot

Do you think parents should be strict

Do you lie to your parents

Do you lie to your friends

Do you lie to yourself

Do you believe you have talent

Do you believe that someone will discover you for your talent without you having to work for it

Do you have a best friend

Do you think friendship is important

Do you believe you have any control over your health

Do the changes of seasons alter the way you feel

Do you brush your teeth in the morning

Do you enjoy staying up late at night

Do you enjoy getting up in the morning

Do you spend money as fast as you get it

Do you enjoy leading other people

Do you enjoy following other people

How do you feel when you make a mistake

How do you feel when others make a mistake

Do you enjoy spending time alone

How do you react to criticism

Do you like people

Do you have more fun when you are alone or when you are in a group

Do you enjoy pretending you are someone else

Are your creative

Do you know how to relax

Do you like animals

Do you enjoy taking risks

Do you like art

Do you like who you are

Are you good at concentrating

Are you afraid of the dark

Do the opinions of others really matter to you

Do you think you are better than other people

Do you feel special

What are your special qualities

Do you think you are smart

Do you consider yourself to be responsible

Do you tend to ignore problems and hope they will go away

Do you get bored often

Do you find that you feel sorry for yourself more than you should

What kind of food do you like to eat

What kind of drinks are your favorites

Do you read books or magazines

What kind of things do you read

Do you slouch or is your posture good

Do you smile more than you frown

Do you enjoy playing sports

How would you describe the clothes you wear

Do you do what your friends do because they are doing it and you would feel left out if you didn't

Do you do things your own way regardless of what your friends think

When you see something happening that is wrong, do you try to stop it

Do you like people who are creative, or do you like people who are calm and orderly

Do you think love is important

Do you believe in love

Do you believe in justice

Do you believe in hard work

Do you believe you are special

Do you believe the choices you have made here reflect who you really are

Some place along your line of answers you will begin to see a pattern emerging. This should be exciting because this pattern is who you are.

The pattern is a bit like making a self-portrait where you draw an oval for a face, and then a shape for a nose, and a shape for a mouth and shapes for eyes. Suddenly something begins to appear from all those shapes that really begins to look like a face, but not just any face, it looks like your face.

And here is the most exciting part about the whole process of our choices **IF YOU DON'T LIKE THE CHOICES YOU ARE MAKING, OR IF YOU DON'T LIKE THE CHOICES YOU HAVE MADE, THEN YOU CAN CHANGE THEM. YOU CAN CHANGE THE DECISIONS YOU MAKE. YOU CAN CHANGE THE PATTERNS YOU ARE MAKING. YOU CAN CHANGE YOUR BELIEFS.**

This is a really important understanding. You can change almost any choice that you have power over.

You can't change your sex, and you can't change your height, and you can't change the color of your eyes or the length of your fingers - but you can change how you 'use' all these things. You can change the way all your beliefs work together. You can change what all your beliefs do and the results they achieve.

You can change what you think of love, for example. You can change what you think of justice. You can change the way you react to fear. You can change your threshold of boredom, and frustration, and even pain. You can change your attitudes, your hopes, your goals, and in this way you can change the choices you make.

When you change your choices you change the answer to the questions of 'who you are'.

The choices belong to you. They are your motivational engine in motion. And that is exciting.

A PLAN
FOR STEERING YOURSELF
IN THE RIGHT
DIRECTION

Chapter 7

FEELINGS ARE DIFFICULT TO EXPLAIN IN WORDS

AN UNLIKELY STORY

Two people who have a really important problem to solve are forced to sit together in a locked room. They must remain in that room until they come up with an acceptable solution. The problem is a common one and requires the efforts of both people to get anything done.

The situation is complicated even further by the fact that neither party speaks the same language. This makes the process of understanding each other extremely difficult.

In order for communication to happen between two people each of them needs to be able to understand what the other is saying. When that understanding isn't there, communication doesn't happen. False ideas become common. Misunderstandings occur with regularity. Answers don't work out or they backfire instead and things become even more difficult as both people find that there is only so much information that can be communicated through grunts and groans and hand gestures.

As all attempts to communicate ideas break down, both sides soon begin to feel increasingly anxious and frustrated. If this state of affairs continues long enough the best that can happen would be for the discussions to eventually break off. If the worst happens both parties will start a circle of anger and violence which could very well escalate into war.

FEELINGS HAVE TROUBLE
UNDERSTANDING THOUGHTS

The situation which was just described may sound a little unlikely, but we really don't have to go very far in order to find similar conditions. We don't have to look any further than right inside our minds to find something almost identical happening.

All people speak at least two languages. One of those languages is made up of words and thoughts, and one is made of feelings. The problem seems to be that neither language really understands the other. The result is that quite often we find our thoughts and feelings fighting each other because they are unable to communicate.

OUR WORD LANGUAGE

Our word language seems to take place mainly in our heads. Because we value our heads as the control center for our bodies anything that takes place there seems to be really important.

The language of words is meant to be slow, and deliberate. Words are meant to be a way of coming to know and understand the world in small pieces. Words are meant to explain things and define things and give labels to things.

We can understand a lot about life when we know that one object is a 'tree', and another object is a 'car', and that another object is an 'apple'. If we didn't have these labels to help us, we might find that we are trying to climb an apple, or drive a tree, or even eat a car, which wouldn't prove too good for out teeth.

Our word language seems friendlier than our feeling language, probably because we can control what we say and think better than we can control how we feel. Because our words seem friendlier, we trust them and use them more confidently.

Unfortunately, by using our word language more than our feeling language, we deny much of the information which our feelings are trying to give us.

OUR FEELING LANGUAGE

Our feeling language seems to take place mainly in our bodies, in the toes and in the arms and in the stomach. Words are not necessary to understand how we feel. When a feeling happens it happens in a rush, and very often we aren't even aware that we are feeling something until it is already happening in our bodies.

When you are afraid, for instance, you know exactly what is happening, and you really don't need words to understand. A feeling sweeps into the body with its message, and it won't go away until it says what it wants to say. That's the reason so many feelings stay around for such a long time, even when we don't want them to, because we haven't figured out what they are trying to say.

By listening to what our feelings are telling us we give the feelings no reason to hang around, as a result they go away until they are needed again.

We do not always listen to our feelings. Because of this they often hang around even when we wish them to fade away. This makes it seem as if we can't control our feelings, and this makes us distrust them. As a result, feelings do not seem as friendly as words and thoughts.

Feelings are difficult to explain in words. Try to explain the feeling of 'love' in words, for example. Poets and writers have been trying to do that for years, and although what they write may sound good in most cases it really ends up making the feeling even more mysterious.

YOUR FEELINGS TALK TO YOU

By not listening to our feelings we ignore a massive amount of information and we ignore a lot of what life is all about.

Suppose you are swinging on vines through a jungle. And suppose you see a promising vine before you. You have only a split second to decide whether it looks strong enough to support your weight. Your feelings tell you instantly whether you should trust the vine or not. Without even knowing what you are doing, your feelings are making all kinds of calculations to help you determine how much you should trust what you see.

If you tried to use words to analyze the safety of the vines ahead of you, you wouldn't get past the first few thoughts before you would no longer be swinging from vines. Instead, you would be falling through the air, and a loud screaming sound would be coming from your mouth.

A BAD CASE OF MISUNDERSTANDING

In the past, people were often so against their feelings that they would actually hurt themselves in order to make their feelings stop. For example, people would fast from food until they got sick, or sleep on a bed of nails, or even whip themselves with leather thongs until they drew blood.

And it worked. While they were in pain they really did forget the other feelings they had, at least for a while. But pain doesn't make feelings go away. Feelings only hide behind the pain until it is gone, and then they come rushing back again.

OUR FEELINGS ARE OUR FRIENDS

If two people who speak different languages really want to work together to solve a common problem they will have to figure out some way of speaking to each other. One of the first things they will have to do is learn to trust each other.

Our feelings and our thinking can work together, and when they do we become much more effective. Feelings are fast and efficient, and words are really good at organizing and making things clear.

Keeping both languages separate is a lot like having the television on without the sound, or the sound on without the picture. Put both the sound and picture on together and the whole thing becomes clearer.

WORKING TOGETHER

Our feelings are tremendously powerful. They have the energy to take us up on an emotional roller coaster and carry us along almost effortlessly. If you don't know about this power, it can be really frightening when it happens. This inclines us to distrust what our feelings have to say.

Suppose you saw a dark shape late at night in the woods that looked an awful lot like a monster. After seeing the shape, your feeling language would look at what is going on and give you a feeling message. You might feel curious, or more likely you would receive a healthy dose of fear. When the fear hits you, you will have a choice: fight the monster, or get away as fast as possible.

Since fighting monsters is not much fun you will probably decide to run away as fast as you can.

However, if you stop yourself long enough to use your thinking language and place labels on what you see, you will probably realize that the monster is no more than a clump of trees and bushes moving in the wind.

By working together your two languages offer you the opportunity of looking at things from two separate directions. Words can provide our feelings with enough information for them to change. Feelings can provide our thinking with enough information to change. Words and feelings can work together to take much clearer pictures of life than either one can while working alone.

WE DON'T STUDY WHAT WE DON'T TRUST

Because we don't understand our feelings, and we don't trust them, we tend not to study them a great deal and so we never learn how to speak the feeling language very well.

For instance, we are told to change our feelings but we aren't told how to do it. We are told to love our neighbor but we aren't told how to do this when our neighbor is a twerp. We are told to be helpful, kind and considerate, but we aren't told how to feel like that when we don't particularly feel much like being helpful, kind and considerate. We are told what to feel, but not how to go about making ourselves feel that way.

Fortunately, learning how to speak the language of our feelings is possible, and it is not as difficult as it might seem.

A SHORT COURSE IN FEELING LANGUAGE

1. Accept that your feelings are trying to talk to you
2. Listen to what your feelings are saying
3. Let your feelings come, listen to them, and they will not hang around when you want them to leave
4. Practice understanding feelings with words, and then words with feelings
5. Learn to trust as many feelings as you can so that you will be able to recall them when you need them
6. Practice replacing one feeling with another until you can do it easily
7. Give yourself permission to feel
8. Feel good about life

Chapter 8

SMILING REALLY IS LOGICAL

Smiling is a subject that we don't discuss enough. When someone smiles at us, we seem to appreciate it. It often makes us feel good and a lot of the time we even smile back, but there doesn't seem to be a lot of discussion about the benefits of smiling.

There is no category for smiling on a report card from school. You might get an 'A' in math, or an 'A' in being a lawyer, but you don't get an 'A' in smiling. We obviously seem to believe that there is more value in learning how to play basketball, or learning how to draw a tree that looks like a tree, than there is in learning how to smile.

Math is a 'hard' skill. It isn't considered hard because it is difficult but because we believe it is important. We also seem to believe that running, track and field events, learning how to be more organized, roller skating and boxing are hard skills.

Learning how to smile, on the other hand, is considered a soft skill. We don't teach people how to smile. We don't work at learning to smile better. Smiling just has not received a lot of attention.

Fortunately, some very solemn scientists have been conducting some very scientific research and taken the very cheerful business of smiling very seriously. Some of the findings of that research are very interesting. Even if experts are not always right in their opinions we can nevertheless learn a great deal about our beliefs and about what motivates us if we listen carefully to what they say.

Paul Ekman taught at a university in California when he told the Los Angeles Times that:

> *"We know that if you have an emotion, it shows on your face. Now we've seen that it goes the other way too. You become what you put on your face....if you laugh at suffering, you don't feel the suffering inside. If your face shows sorrow, you do tend to feel it inside."*

Ekman is saying that if you feel pain, or if you feel down and depressed, simply by changing the shape of your face into a smile you can quite possibly change how you feel inside.

Research is finding that there are as many as 21 different types of smile, and that each type makes us feel a different type of emotion.

I personally doubt that there are 21 different ways of smiling. Humans love to pretend they know what they are talking about by using lots of words and lots of statistics, but that does not mean we really know what we are talking about. The important point is not how many different smiles there are, but what it does for us and how it helps us.

We smile as a result of different kinds of things happening to us. It is an expression of something we feel inside.

The question is, if we smile as a result of an inside feeling, can we turn the whole process around? Can we make the tail wag the dog rather than have the dog wag the tail the way it usually does? Can we really use a smile to change the way we feel?

Robert Zajonc did research on smiling at the University of Michigan. His findings suggest that smiling changes some of the veins which run from the face directly back into the brain. Smiles open some of these veins and shut others down. Zajonc suggests that this stimulates the brain and causes it to produce chemicals called endorphins. These endorphins act on us to help us feel really good. According to Zajonc, when you smile the endorphins you produce cause you to feel good. Nothing could be simpler. The tail can wag the dog.

If you don't believe what Zajonc says, try an experiment. Think about something happy, and smile. Or think about something really funny, and smile. Let your whole body be involved, not just with a phony, plastic smile. Phony plastic smiles make you feel phony and plastic.

Real smiles make you feel bigger and stronger and healthier. Small, nervous ones make you feel as if you are small and nervous, as if you have made a mistake. Real smiles bring the endorphins while pretend ones bring pretence.

Patricia Russel did some research on the subject at Allegheny College that was really interesting. Her research suggested that a smile or a frown changes what we see and how we feel about life.

Russel had two groups of people watch a sad movie. One group smiled while they watched the movie, and the other group frowned while they watched. Russel found that the group that smiled did not find the sad movie nearly as sad as the group that frowned. Not only that, the group that frowned felt sad much longer than the group that smiled.

What this means is that we really can change the way we feel simply by smiling. What a tremendous belief to have. What a tremendous motivational tool this gives us. If you want to feel better a simple smile can help lead the way.

Now, smiling won't take away all the pain. Nor will it help you feel really great when you are feeling really down. But it will remove some of the pain's hard edge, and it will take some of the depression out of being depressed.

Smiling is not only good for you it is also good for other people. Smiles can spread easily from person to person if given a chance. The more open you are to smiling, the more frequently you will catch yourself doing it, and the more frequently you will find others doing the same thing. Smiling is a habit, and we can learn that habit with very little trouble.

If someone yells at you, smile back, and the yell doesn't mean as much as it might have. If someone does something mean to you, smile, and watch the way it improves how you feel. If you bump your leg or stub your toe, smile, and watch how the hurt is unable to get a really good hold of you.

Smiling is so catchy that if you try it enough times you will one day find yourself smiling in situations which at one time would have made you feel bad, or angry, or guilty or even afraid.

We all have natural resources right inside of us. We can mine those resources any time we want, and use what we mine to make life seem brighter.

But we carry a never ending supply of rocks inside of us as well, and reaching for a rock or reaching for a smile are choices we make. Mining for smiles rather than rocks is a habit we can teach ourselves. Throwing a smile is better than throwing a rock any day.

A PLAN
FOR STEERING YOURSELF
IN THE RIGHT
DIRECTION

THE SNAKE GOES HISS THE DOG GOES WOOF AND THE COMPUTER SAYS THAT DOES NOT COMPUTE

Question: Using the qualities listed below, identify the following mystery object:

- *It is smaller than a loaf of bread.*
- *It is about the size of a small coconut.*
- *It weighs about 3 pounds or about 1300 grams.*
- *It knows a lot of jokes.*
- *It can figure out math problems.*
- *It can see things that aren't there.*
- *It is an expert in chemistry.*
- *It has anywhere from 15 billion to 100 billion little parts.*
- *It remembers faces.*
- *It is very wrinkled.*
- *It doesn't have a medical degree but it is an incredible healer.*
- *It uses light waves and sound waves to gather information.*
- *There is a limit to the things it can do, but that limit has not yet been defined.*
- *It can create things which have never existed.*
- *It is about 500 million years old give or take a few million years?*

Answer: Make fists with both your hands. Place your fists together so that the knuckles touch and the palms touch. The mystery object is about the same size and shape as your joined fists. The object is <u>your brain</u>.

A BRIEF HISTORY OF THE HUMAN BRAIN[1]

Our brain is really something extraordinarily special and we do not give it enough credit for what it does for us.

Without a brain you would be unable to read this. Without a brain I would be unable to write this. Without a brain there would be no human thought, no family, no religion, no factories, no television, no bubble gum, no human life as we know it.

No doctor can do as much as your brain can do for you. When you are sick your brain directs the process of making you well again. When you are well your brain works to keep you that way even without you being aware of what is going on inside of you.

Your brain communicates with your heart and lungs and other organs by manufacturing chemicals we call hormones and then sending these hormones throughout your body as messengers. One chemical will tell us to run, another will tell us to freeze, and still another might tell our hearts to speed up so that we can act faster.

Your brain has such a fantastic memory that it can see a face and remember it fifty years later in spite of the changes which have taken place. It learns so well that eventually it can do things without having to think about what it is doing, like ride a bike or drive a car or eat a pizza.

It can be really flexible and learn a whole bunch of different things. It can take risks, enjoy new things in life and be curious about what life is all about. This way of using the brain leads to excitement and challenge.

Your brain can also be told to be inflexible, learn only certain kinds of things which won't make you challenge your beliefs, and never try anything new or creative. This way of using the brain is almost guaranteed to lead to boredom.

Your brain has the ability to store an amount of information equal to about 11 billion encyclopedia pages. This is a staggering amount of knowledge which should have the potential to help humans work out their problems with very little trouble.

Information is supposed to reduce anxiety, and a massive amount of information should reduce anxiety to zero. The fact that humans are still poor at solving problems tells us there is something about the human brain which prevents it from working as well as it could.

THE BRAIN AS UNDERACHIEVER

On the whole, brains tend to be underachievers. They seldom work up to their potential and in many instances actually seem to be fighting themselves, creating roadblocks rather than preventing them. To understand some of the reasons for this internal disagreement we need to follow our brains about 500 million years into the past.

If we could look inside a dinosaur's head we would find a brain about the same shape as the brain now found in modern reptiles such as lizards, alligators, turtles and snakes. Compared to other animals without similar brains this primitive brain was very powerful. It allowed reptiles to eat better, to decide on who was the boss reptile, to defend territory, and to take care of the body's needs more successfully.

During the next 150 million years a newer and more powerful brain grew over the primitive reptilian brain. This newer brain gave the animals which possessed it a tremendous number of new ways to live more effectively in the world. Animals such as rats, kangaroos, rabbits and horses have similar brains.

With the mammalian brain in place animals could now feel emotions such as sadness, affection, pleasure and love. This allowed mammals to live in groups without constant fighting so that they could combine their efforts to increase success.

Wolves hunting in a pack is a good example of how combined efforts makes the group stronger and more powerful than an individual.

About 50 million years ago a new brain succeeded in growing over the primitive mammalian brain which had itself grown over the even more primitive reptilian brain so long ago. This new brain, called the neo-cortex, allowed for inventive and more successful ways of getting along with the world. Things could now be thought out logically, rationally, problems could now be solved without emotion.

The fact that this is being written on a computer is an example of the overwhelming success the new brain has achieved in some areas. We are able to talk over distances, walk on the moon, and even look deep inside the human body without injuring any of the parts. These accomplishments have all been made possible by the neo-cortex.

SOMETIMES THREE BRAINS ARE NOT BETTER THAN ONE

In spite of our incredible brains we continue to have problems controlling our emotions and doing what we know needs to be done. Knowing that a project is due a week from tomorrow does not prevent us from feeling that we should put it off until tomorrow. Knowing what is right does not always help us do what is right.

Logic tells us one thing at the same time as other messages are flashing in our minds and providing us with other ways of looking at things. But where do these messages come from? Why do we do things which we shouldn't do even while we know we shouldn't be doing them?

As previously mentioned, when the mammalian brain grew it did not throw away the reptilian brain, it kept the older brain and simply grew over it. Using what is already there makes a lot of sense and is called learning.

When it came time for the neo-cortex to grow it didn't throw away the primitive reptilian and mammalian brains either. Instead, it simply grew over the old brains and set about gaining control of the skills they had already developed.

The human brain is as powerful as it is because it can use the abilities of the primitive brains. But it is those exact qualities which made our brains so powerful in the past, which also cause us so many problems in the present.

THE SNAKE GOES 'HISS'

Have you ever taken a snake for a walk? Or have you ever played 'chase the stick' with a lizard? The reason you haven't is because reptiles don't do those kinds of things. Their primitive brains know only certain ways to behave and stay alive, and that is the way they live from birth to death.

Reptiles don't have to think a lot to be aggressive because that is built right into their brains. They don't have to think a lot to be quickly angered. They don't worry a lot about whether they are right or wrong.

When a reptile has a problem, the cause of the problem is always someone else, and blame is a big part of their lives. They don't have to think a lot in order to want to survive. They simply survive. So, don't get in their way, and if you do it is always your fault.

Reptiles are not famous for sharing what they have. The whole idea of being greedy makes sense to a reptile because that means they will eat and survive. Looking out for #1 makes perfect sense to a reptile because the reptile doesn't have the thinking equipment to realize that better ways exist. When the snake goes 'hiss' it makes perfect sense to the snake because the snake knows no other way.

Humans don't think very highly of reptile qualities such as aggression, anger, blaming, greed, and stinginess, however we don't have to look very far inside ourselves in order to find that those negative reptile traits are human traits as well.

THE DOG GOES "WOOF"

Mammals feed their young milk. That is one of the telling differences between reptiles and mammals. Even if we didn't know this, it would still be easy to tell the difference between a reptile and a mammal by the way they act.

Mammals know what love means, while a reptile knows nothing at all about it. Loyalty and faithfulness have no place in the reptile world where every reptile looks out for itself.

Mammals know what it means to work for the common good. They are even able to learn, and this fact alone makes them a lot closer to humans than reptiles could ever be.

Over the millions of years that it took for mammals to change from their reptile ancestors, they developed a new way of understanding the world around them which reptiles were incapable of appreciating.

Mammals invented feelings and this allowed them to think without really having advanced mental equipment. When a mammal feels fear it does not need to be able to think a lot to figure out what is happening. When a mammal feels love it does not have to think a lot to figure out what is going on. Loyalty, friendship, belonging, pride - emotions help mammals live richer, fuller, more in-depth lives.

THE NEO-CORTEX SAYS
"THAT DOES NOT COMPUTE"

When the neo-cortex came along it brought with it a whole new way of looking at the world, and it is here where many of our modern problems began. Even though the three brains are all connected together, they have trouble communicating with each other.

Your new brain doesn't really work like a computer, but if we think about it as a computer it will help us understand the way it really might work.

You can program your neo-cortex just like you can program a computer. Your neo-cortex stores information just like a computer, and it tends to be logical, just like a computer.

The reptilian brain knows nothing about emotion, and the mammalian brain knows nothing about logic, and the neo-cortex can't figure out where all the strange messages are coming from. The snake goes "hiss" and the dog goes "woof" and the computer says "that does not compute".

A dog does not understand a snake, and a snake does not understand a dog, and the neo-cortex can't figure out what the fuss is all about. That leaves us with a lot of conflicting thoughts and feelings, and that is why we are often so confused.

A BRAIN TO BLAME

When you complain or accuse or act without thinking, you are probably listening to your old brains and being influenced by their primitive ways.

When you need to be boss, or you get angry because things aren't going your way, or you feel that people are wrong just because they are different somehow, then you are probably listening to your really old brains and finding limits to your ability to think logically.

When you defend yourself and your actions, even though you are wrong, and you know you are wrong, then you are listening to your old brains. When you feel hate or rage or jealousy or envy, and you really don't want to, then you are listening to your old brains.

On the other hand, you are listening to your new brain:

- *when you deliberately try to forgive others in spite of the fact that you don't feel that you want to forgive them.*
- *when you try to be fair even though you don't really feel like it.*
- *when you try to learn from your mistakes.*
- *when you stop yourself from lashing out at people who disagree with you.*
- *when you talk out problems rather than hold in bad feelings.*
- *when you listen to your feelings and your intellect and make a decision based upon both.*
- *when you do things which make sense even though you find that you have urges inside you which want you to act differently.*

Because of the conflicts of our three brain system we are not entirely responsible for the thoughts we keep thinking and the feelings we keep feeling.

In our heads we have urges which go all the way back to when our ancestors were dinosaurs. When you know these urges are going to come you will be better prepared for their arrival. When you know that these urges won't go away just because you use your neo-cortex to will them away, then you won't feel bad when your efforts don't work.

Next time you have a problem, ask your new brain what your old brain wants, and make your decision based upon the information you receive. You will live a far more effective life. If you try hard enough, a "hiss" and a "woof" will compute, and make sense doing it.

[1]*The basic theory presented in this chapter stems from the work done by James W. Papez and Paul D. MacLean.*

Chapter 10

WHAT YOU DO DOES MAKE A DIFFERENCE

What you do makes a difference. It really does.

Put your hands together as if you were praying. With your hands still out in front of you, move them apart slowly.

What your hands now represent is the difference between what you want, and what you get.

Hands which are far apart represent a great difference between what you want and what you get.

GAP SIZE	CONSEQUENCE	FEELING
small	in control	strong
getting bigger	losing control	anxious
large	lost control	helpless

When the gap is small, or closed entirely, we feel right, we feel in control, we feel on top of things. When the gap is large we feel wrong, at odds with everything, and we will try very hard to find some way to close it up.

We continually makechoices according to the 'gap' we feel. The lack of control we feel from a large gap causes us to distrust our ability to achieve success and makes the gap even harder to close. A large gap also means that there are many choices which could be taken, and this serves to make the problem even more complex.

Let's look at an example. Suppose you wanted to get an 'A' grade in science. When it came to the test you did poorly, and you actually failed. Now, the difference between what you want, an 'A', and what you actually received, an 'E', is very large. Your hands would have to be very far apart to show this difference.

The difference tends to make you want to act in some way which will cause that gap to close. You are going to want to do something, and what you are going to do will depend on a lot of factors.

If you feel special, then you will act to close the gap in ways which will raise your level of confidence. You will be less concerned about 'failure' and self-doubt, and your subsequent efforts with be focused on the problem rather than how you feel about the problem.

By believing you have the ability to achieve an 'A', you give yourself more time to concentrate on fine tuning your solutions and less time doubting your ability to be right. You will not have a high level of helplessness and learning will come easier.

When the gap is large, your tendency is to feel that you lack control, that you are helpless. As a consequence, your choices tend to agree with how you feel, and the result of this is that you are not as effective as you could be.

A large gap means that a considerable number of choices are available to act as possible solutions. Some possibilities will be effective, but a lot will only seem to be constructive and will actually cause more harm than good.

You might get nervous about failing and get so pumped up with stress that studying becomes almost painful. When this happens you have provided yourself with a perfectly good reason for not studying.

You might come to believe that science doesn't really matter and decide to watch television rather than studying. You might feel better while watching television, but very little of what you watch will have anything to do with science, and you will be unprepared for the next test.

You might also decide to fill the science gap with anger, or you might decide to blame the failure on others rather than yourself. This takes a considerable amount of pressure off you, and at the same time accounts for your bad performance while leaving you almost blameless.

You might also decide to get depressed and turn yourself off rather than face up to the responsibility of working hard. You might even decide that the easiest route to passing is by cheating on the next test.

Large differences tend to keep themselves going. Because a large difference makes you a little frantic, you might try to fill the gap with the first solution you find, even a solution which is ineffective or which you know probably won't work. The results tend to keep the difference as large as it originally was and often serve to make the difference even larger.

Fortunately, everything we have talked about so far is the negative side of the difference. There is a positive side as well, one that is extremely important. If you use it properly it will help you figure out some of the choices you should make.

You know a difference has opened up and is operating when:

• you feel a sudden sinking sensation in your stomach

• you feel really nervous

• you are anxious or feeling a great deal of stress

• you feel jealous or envious

• you really dislike someone or something for no apparent reason

Knowing that a difference exists is the first step in helping yourself make life run easier. Figuring out how to close the gap is the next step.

The last step is to decide how effective your actions really are. Too often we act in the hope that an action, any action at all, will fill the gap and make us feel better. But pretending something is being done when it really isn't does not help close the gap and actually makes things worse when nothing gets better.

Let's say you have an important exam tomorrow, you aren't really prepared for it, and your favorite television show is on. What do you do? The gap between what you want, and what you should be doing is large, and you feel that difference. The pressure is on.

Your choices are limited. You could fill the gap by studying for a few minutes and pretending you know the material so that you could watch your show. And when you fail the test you can fill that gap by blaming it on the teacher.

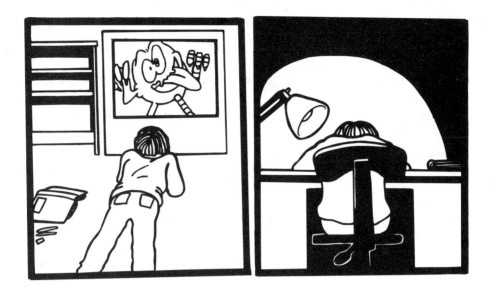

On the other hand, you could study hard and not watch the television, and as a result do well on the important exam. You have closed the gap, but this time you are doing yourself good.

Knowing about the gap can help us get along better with people. When you know a person has a big difference between wanting something and getting something, you can conclude that person will act to close the gap. Some people will try to close that gap at your expense. When you know it is a possibility, or you see it happening, you can then act to stop it.

When you see other people trying to close their gaps and you can see them struggling, this gives you an opportunity to act in ways which will help them. Helping people close their gaps and feel better as a result can help you feel better about who you are.

When we think about all the gaps and differences in our lives it is wise to remember that not all problems can be solved or even need to be solved. Life is often so complicated that we forget how wonderful and magical it really is, problems and all. One of the best ways to close any gaps we might discover is to realize the value of life and to stop taking ourselves so seriously.

Many of our problems are not life threatening, regardless of how serious they might seem at the time. Some of the gaps we feel will simply close by themselves, without any help from us. However, this is not an excuse for inaction. The gaps which won't disappear on their own must be dealt with before they get so large they become impossible to close.

In the final analysis what we do does make a difference. Unfortunately, it is true that what we don't do makes a difference as well. The difference is up to us.

Chapter 11

THE GLASS IS EITHER HALF FULL OR HALF EMPTY

Imagine that you are hanging onto the end of a long rope which is running down the side of a high cliff. You are swaying back and forth. Your arms are getting tired.

When you get enough courage to look down, you see the rocks and boulders of the gorge bottom far under your feet. The rocks and boulders look hard. They look very sharp. They look like teeth.

Each time your feet swing you get a terrible sinking sensation in the pit of your stomach, a sensation that sweeps through your body as your hands tighten even more fearfully on the rope.

High above you in the sky a couple of turkey vultures are wheeling and circling on the wind currents, looking down at you with hungry eyes.

If you look up to the top of the cliff you will see someone holding the rope. That person literally holds your life in his or her hands. If the person grows tired and the rope slips a little, you will fall downwards in a series of jerks. Each jerk will make it harder for the person to hold the rope. If the person lets go, you will drop like a stone.

The fear is that there will come a time when all the little jerks will add up into one jerk too many, and the rope will be released, and you will fall and fall.

It is said that there is really no difference between being a pessimist or being an optimist. It is said that pessimism and optimism are just two ways of looking at life, no more than that. According to this way of thinking both ways of looking at life produce the same quality of life.

But if this were true, and you really were hanging over a gorge by a rope, would you really want a pessimist holding you up?

A pessimist is a person who thinks that the worst will happen. An optimist is a person who thinks the best will happen.

A pessimist is negative, always ready to accept the worst because the worst has been expected, and probably expected for a long time.

A pessimist is always ready to give up, or give in, or throw in the towel. If you are a pessimist, why bother hanging on when you are certain that the worst is going to happen no matter what you do?

On the other hand, an optimist looks more for the positive than the negative. An optimist searches through the negatives to find the positives. The positives are always there, but sometimes they are so covered in negatives that it requires work to find them.

So, who would you rather have holding the end of the rope? Someone who expects the worst to happen, or someone who is convinced that a positive solution can be found for almost any situation?

Most people who enjoy life would agree that if they really were hanging from a long rope over a deep gorge it would be important that the person who was holding the rope expected positive results to happen.

If you look for the bad to happen, and you look for it long enough, then it will almost always happen. That is part of the logic of life. If you look for the bad hard enough, you can get so caught up in that kind of thinking that you might not be capable of seeing the good when it does come along.

If you look for the good to happen, if you actually spend your mental effort looking for ideas which might work, you strengthen your position every day. Making things work becomes a frame of mind, a mind set, a way of looking at life. When life works in the general sense, life also tends to work in the small things as well.

When you look at life and at problems in an optimistic, positive way, then the information you receive tends to become empowering and it makes you stronger.

If you remove half of the water from a full glass of water, how much water remains? Is the glass half empty, or is it half full?

There is mathematical proof that the glass is half full. You see, if you take half of something, there is always half remaining, no matter how small it gets to be, it never disappears.

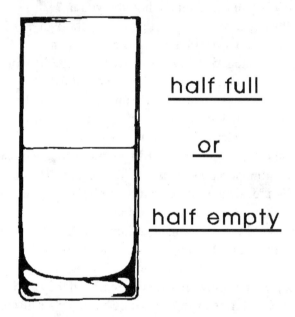

If you walked half of the distance between here and the closest wall, and then walked half of the remaining distance, and then half of that remaining distance, you would in theory never reach the wall because there would always be the remaining half left.

Each way of looking at life sets up separate possibilities. If the glass is half empty, and your view is pessimistic, then you are on the way toward depletion, on the way to running down. Even before it is over, it is already over. It is already half empty even before it is completely empty.

If the glass is full, then it is never over until it is over. If you look at life as an optimist then you will never really know life as a defeat. Nothing will keep you down longer than it takes for you to get up and dust yourself off.

When you look at life in this way, you give yourself the ability to tolerate your mistakes and your failures long enough for you to understand how to prevent future mistakes.

Fortunately, in real life most of us will never have to worry about hanging by a rope over a gorge, or about who is holding us. That type of thing isn't a big part of real life.

In our minds, however, our beliefs hold us over a gorge and there is always the chance that we will let ourselves go and fall down. In our minds there is always the chance that the next risk, the next mistake, the next failure will be our last failure and will determine whether we fall or not, and how far, and even how fast.

If we are optimists we will always be able to reach out and grab the rope again. We will always be able to stop the fall and climb back up repeatedly.

A pessimist does not have the same opportunities for success. A pessimist does not have the same store of hope, or faith, or belief, or strength. A pessimist does not see the point in reaching out, or trying to stop the fall. After all, what would be the point?

You always have a choice. There is something positive in nearly every situation, no matter what the predicament. Sometimes it is hidden, but it is there. To find it you first have to look for it. To find it you need to believe it is there, that the glass is half full, that things will turn out for the best, and they will.

Believe it. They really will.

A PLAN
FOR STEERING YOURSELF
IN THE RIGHT
DIRECTION

Chapter 12

RUDOLPH THE RED NOSED REINDEER LEARNED HOW TO REFRAME

The story of Rudolph the Red Nosed Reindeer is a story that has been around for a long time. On the surface it looks like a very simple tale about a reindeer with an odd nose. If you look at the story closely, however, if you examine what is being talked about, you can see that it is an excellent example of how learning can make our lives better.

Rudolph lived with Santa and the elves and all the other reindeer up at the North Pole. Although Santa liked him, poor Rudolph was not well liked by the other reindeer. You see, Rudolph was normal in all respects except one - where the other reindeer had regular noses, Rudolph had one that was not only really big, it was also really red.

Rudolph's nose was so red that when he walked around in the dark it looked as if he was wearing a lantern on his head. All of the other reindeer made fun of him and called him names and they wouldn't let him join in any of the games they played.

This made poor Rudolph very unhappy. He didn't have any friends. He didn't have anyone to talk to. Because of this he did not see himself as a very valuable reindeer, and the pictures of himself that he carried in his mind were not very flattering.

When he thought about wanting to do things, like make friends, or win at the reindeer games, or do well in school, he would hear voices laughing at him inside his head telling him that he simply could not do what he wanted to do.

Life was very sad for Rudolph and he walked around with his head down and tucked between his front legs trying to hide the glow of his nose. He never once thought to question what the other reindeer were saying, or ask himself whether they were right when they made fun of him.

Rudolph carried a picture in his mind which explained how much success he should expect whenever he wanted to try something new. The picture he carried of himself was not that flattering because he let the other reindeer tell him what the picture should look like.

When they laughed at him and called him names he let the pictures of himself look funny and odd. When the other reindeer made fun of his red nose Rudolph made the mental picture of his nose look ridiculous and stupid.

But what right did those reindeer have to pass judgments?

Actually, the other reindeer had no right to pass judgments about Rudolph's nose. That did not stop them. They passed judgment anyway.

The other reindeer showed a very poor quality of thinking. They did not stop to think about how Rudolph might feel when they made fun of him. They didn't stop to think about how he might feel when they refused to play with him or let him join in their games. They just refused, and didn't concern themselves about his feelings.

So the picture Rudolph had framed in his head, which explained for him how much value he had and how much he should trust himself, was not a very happy one. When he visualized himself playing with other reindeer the pictures were always sad ones. When he looked at many of the other pictures he carried in his head he found that they were also sad, and that they didn't have very confident frames around them either.

When the other reindeer saw Rudolph as different they treated him as different. Poor Rudolph used the way he was treated to help him decide that he probably was different, and this made him feel even worse.

When something is different in this world it often can mean danger is near. One of the best ways of dealing with something that is different and possibly dangerous is by avoiding it. Which is exactly what the reindeer did to Rudolph. They avoided him. And because Rudolph did not know any better he decided the other reindeer were right, and he was wrong.

Santa, or the elves, or Rudolph's parents should have explained that it was his choice to believe what the other reindeer said, and that he didn't have to make that choice. Someone should have told him that feeling bad because others did not like him was his choice, and that he did not have to feel bad.

Fortunately, life did give Rudolph another chance to see his own value. It gave him an opportunity to reframe the pictures he carried in his mind. It gave him an opportunity to make new choices about old ways of knowing things. And this changed his life. It changed the way he saw himself. In return, it changed the way life saw him.

One Christmas night Santa hitched his team of reindeer up to the sleigh and prepared to take off for his yearly round of deliveries. A raging storm had developed and forced a delay in take-off. As time went by and the hour grew late Santa began to pace nervously back and forth. What was he going to do? The storm had made it impossible to see where he was going. How could he deliver his presents to all the girls and boys of the world when he couldn't see where he was going?

Of course, poor Rudolph was standing away from the action, with his head down, looking sad and feeling sad. He didn't feel he belonged and so he acted as if he really didn't belong by standing aside. After a while everyone took it for granted that Rudolph did not belong.

The story is a little vague here depending on which version of events you read. Either Santa suddenly saw Rudolph's nose glowing in the dark and lighting up the storm, or Rudolph suddenly discovered his own potential for lighting up the dark. In either case the results were the same.

Santa and the sled reindeer helped hitch Rudolph to the front of the sleigh and that ugly red nose suddenly became a blazing red beacon capable of lighting up the darkness of the storm.

The moment Rudolph could see his ugly red nose as a valuable sled light he became a different reindeer. At that moment the pictures he carried in his mind changed. His posture straightened. His eyes lost their glaze. His

shoulders became strong and square. He felt new energy course through his body. He felt his heart beating stronger, with more pride.

Rudolph was not just different, he was different with a bang. When he learned to reframe his own value, his own usefulness, this helped him reframe everything else. As soon as he was able to frame what he knew about his nose in a different way he began to see himself in an entirely new and different way.

Those nasty reindeer who had made fun of him before were now behind him one hundred percent. Rudolph was doing the directing, he was doing the steering. He was special because while Santa was depending on the other reindeer in general, he was depending on Rudolph in particular. All this made Rudolph stronger, and he flew faster, and his nose burned brighter, and he became even more effective and more useful and more successful.

Have you ever seen carpenters build a house? First they begin with a frame made of concrete and wood and plywood. The final shape of the house is determined by this frame. If the frame provides for two rooms on the main floor, and four rooms on the second floor, that is the way the house will end up with two rooms on the first floor and four on the second.

Rudolph didn't build houses, but he did build little beliefs in his mind, and he took pictures of them. After a while he had so many mental pictures saved up they were powerful enough to set all kinds of limits on how he could behave.

A mansion can't be built on the frame of a bungalow and a big truck can't be built on the frame of a small sports car. And Rudolph could not build a feeling of self-value and self-worth and high self-esteem on internal pictures of low value, low belief, and low self-confidence.

When Rudolph reframed his beliefs about who he was and the kinds of things he was capable of doing in life, he gained a lot of new information, and this helped him set new goals and make new plans.

By reframing he took apart the old structure of being different and having an ugly nose. He then built a whole new picture of having a beautifully useful and effective nose, a picture which made him feel special and unique. Once the old frame was gone he could make new choices.

You can do what Rudolph did. You can learn to see yourself in a new way. You can learn to change the frame you use to see yourself. You can make different choices, build new frames, and change the entire structure of your life. What a reindeer can do, you can do too.

A PLAN
FOR STEERING YOURSELF
IN THE RIGHT
DIRECTION

Chapter 13

LIFE IS A SERIES OF PROBLEMS BOUND TOGETHER BY SOLUTIONS

There are a lot of mysteries in the world. One of them is why people believe it is more important to memorize the capital of Peru than it is to learn how to solve real life problems.

When life threatens to break, or when it actually does break, knowing that the capital of Peru is Lima is going to be absolutely no help at all.

When an enraged bull is charging down at you in top gear, with steam pouring from his nostrils, how much good will it do to shout, "Lima, Lima! The capital of Peru is Lima."

For some reason, our schools seem to believe the most important problems we should learn how to solve are the ones which have to do with mathematics or science.

If Melissa has four oranges, and Tony eats one orange, and Li eats another one of the oranges, how many oranges would Melissa have left? In terms of math the answer to the problem is simple. Melissa would have two oranges left.

But Melissa's real problem is not math. Her real problem is not science. Melissa's real problem has to do with how willing she is to share her oranges. What if Tony and Li don't ask for the oranges, but decide to take them instead? How does Melissa handle this problem? Knowing that she will have only two oranges left is only the beginning of the problem rather than the solution.

Problems aren't just mathematical or scientific. Problems are about life. And problems are not always fair, or logical.

There is a really wonderful cartoon about a little boy trying to wrap a package in sticky tape. The problem is that the more tape he pulls from the roll, the more difficult it becomes to place the tape on the package because it all wants to stick on him instead.

In the end, all the tape is gone from the roll, the boy has taped his hands and feet to the package, the whole thing looks like a mess, and the boy is looking really puzzled. It is then that he arrives at a really fantastic conclusion, for he finds that the major problem with problems is that they always lead to more problems.

There is a major lesson in that cartoon. Problem solving is a never ending business. As soon as you manage to fix one problem another problem shows up. That is the way of the world. One problem follows the other in a never ending procession as if they were holding hands.

If you don't know how to solve a problem you had better learn, because not knowing how to stop problems will not prevent them from coming. Problems never stop coming.

From the time you wake in the morning until the time you go back to sleep at night you continue to encounter problems of every sort and type and variety. Most problems need to be solved in some way or life will simply break and not continue.

Should I get up or go back to sleep? What side of the bed should I get out of? Should I wear my jeans to school or should I skip school today? Should I brush my teeth or just pretend to make mom happy? And on and on and on and on. It is just like a television ad that lacks creativity: no problem too big, no problem too small, life has them all.

In fact, if you wanted to define life in a way that will help you fix it when it breaks then you could say that:

LIFE IS A SERIES OF INTERCONNECTED PROBLEMS

➡ problem ➡ problem ➡ problem ➡ problem ➡ problem ➡

If you wanted to get to know life a little better, perhaps understand a little better how life is put together, then you could say that life is not only a series of interconnected problems, but also that life is a series of interconnected solutions.

LIFE IS A SERIES OF INTERCONNECTED PROBLEMS & SOLUTIONS

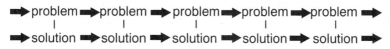

➡ problem ➡ problem ➡ problem ➡ problem ➡ problem ➡
    | | | | |
➡ solution ➡ solution ➡ solution ➡ solution ➡ solution ➡

The solution you have for one problem will determine the kind of problems which will pop up next. Problems and solutions are connected together. The choices you make now will determine the choices you will be able to make tomorrow.

Suppose, for example, you are with a friend walking down a street and talking. Now, this friend bends down and picks a bunch of flowers from a flower garden. And then the friend looks at you and demands that you pick a bunch of flowers too to prove just how much of a friend you really are.

Your problem: do you pick the flowers, and conform to what your friend did, or do you listen to your own reason which says that it is unwise and illegal to pick from somebody's garden for no reason at all.

If your choice is to pick the flowers, then certain other problems will rise up to confront you. The owner of the flowers might chase you, the owner might have a dog that will chase you, the police might chase you, or your own conscience might chase you because you know that you have done something which you shouldn't have done.

If you choose not to pick the flowers then that may give rise to another problem. Your friend may call you names, or maybe even exclude you from the group.

In order to really learn what a problem is all about you need to examine the whole problem as carefully as you can. You need to decide what the results of your solution will mean now, after you do it, and what it might mean down the road a bit in the future.

You need to ask yourself, "If I do this, what will happen?" And you need to take the time to really think about the answers you give yourself.

If you pick flowers that don't belong to you just to please your friend you would solve a problem in the here and now. But you would also probably find more unwanted and unnecessary problems coming at you as a result of your action.

No matter how much you think over your solutions, you will find that some of them will work out, some won't change anything at all, and some will make things worse. If you look closely you will find that the quality of your life exactly matches the quality of your solutions. This makes it extremely important that you think about the consequences of what you do before you act.

THE QUALITY OF THE SOLUTIONS TO YOUR PROBLEMS DETERMINES THE QUALITY OF YOUR LIFE

There is another way of saying the same thing: The choices you make now will determine the choices you will be able to make in the future.

THE CHOICES YOU MAKE NOW DETERMINE THE CHOICES YOU WILL BE ABLE TO MAKE IN THE FUTURE

Once you choose to pick the flowers you will set a chain of problems in motion which will not give you a lot of choices. If the owner or his dog chase you for picking the flowers you have a really limited number of choices you are then able to use to solve your problem.

If you choose to continually overeat, then you will one day be over-weight, and the problems which will confront you will be a direct result of the eating actions you have taken.

You have to be a bit of a fortune teller in order to know what is going to happen next after you choose a solution. Your guesses will be wrong more than they are right, but if you do a good job of forecasting, and if you get even 40% right, you will have joined the ranks of excellent problem solvers.

Baseball Hall of Famers who achieve astonishing 300 and 400 batting averages are successful at the plate only 30 or 40 percent of the time. This means they are unsuccessful 60 to 70 percent of the time. This clearly shows that what is important is not the failures, but the successes.

I wish I had known that when I was young. There were times in my life when I was unhappy and I felt that there was nothing I could do to change that unhappiness. When I look back at those periods it is easy to see that the solutions I chose for my problems weren't really very good ones. As a result the quality of my life during those times was not very good.

I know now that I should have stepped up to the plate a few more times to see if I could hit a few problems over the fence. But no one ever told me that would be a good idea, and I wasn't able to figure it out for myself.

LISTS, SECRETS AND SOLUTIONS

If you look carefully you will find that your problems hold secrets. When you think about it those secrets are why your problems are still problems. In order to come up with solutions you will need to discover what those secrets are. You will need to find the problem within the problem.

Looking for the secret problem is a bit like a treasure hunt where you know the treasure is buried somewhere in the big hill in front of you, but it could be in any one of a thousand different places, and you don't know where to start digging.

Solutions do not just pop up from nowhere. Everything needs to be constructed from some kind of material, and solutions to problems are no different. The construction material we use to build solutions is 'informa-tion' and 'intuition'.

What is your intuition? No one really knows. Your intuition is some part of your mind that creates or makes solutions. You feed information into one end, and eventually a pile of stuff comes out the other end. If you look through that pile of stuff you will find some stuff that looks a lot like answers, and some stuff that looks a lot like junk.

In order to solve problems what you need to do is collect as much information from as many places as you can. Keep looking for the secret within the secret, the problem within the problem. Give your intuition something to munch on. The more it has to munch on, the more chance you have of coming up with valuable choices.

Making lists is the easiest method of collecting information that has ever been invented. It is really good for organizing information, and this helps you understand what the information really looks like.

If you want to find the treasure, or find the problem within the problem, make a list of places to look. If you aren't sure where to look, make a list of things you should look for in order to find the best place to look. If you aren't certain of the best way to make a list, make a list of possible ways of making lists.

Lists are magic. Your intuition loves lists. With a good information list you can build a solution to any problem in your life.

To show you how valuable lists are let me give you a list of list topics you could use in order to gather information to feed your intuition.

A LIST OF POSSIBLE LISTS

- A list of things you should do today.
- A list of things you shouldn't do today.
- A list of goals.
- A list of your good points.
- A list of things you are good at.
- A list of things you like to do.
- A list of problems you have.
- A list of problems you don't have.
- A list of solutions for your problems.
- A list of why your solutions won't work.
- A list of actions which make you feel good.
- A list of people who are your problems.
- A list of people who are solutions for you.
- A list of lists you could make.

Most of the dirt you dig up while hunting for buried treasure will have only a limited value. The more dirt you pile up the closer you will get to the treasure, but you won't really know the value of the dirt until you have dug it up and sorted through it.

In the same way the information you dig up won't all be worthwhile. A lot of it will be junk. You'll want to throw most of it away eventually but you won't really know its value until you have it organized in front of you.

A list of information works wonderfully to connect the obvious problem to the secret problem, and to give your intuition some room to move around.

Knowing that the capital of Peru is Lima will not help solve many problems. On the other hand, knowing how to find the problem within the problem, the secret within the secret can make the difference between a life of quality and a life of uncertainty and helplessness.

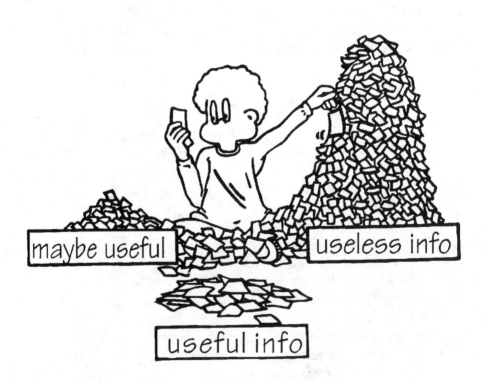

Chapter 14

YOUR REFS HAVE THEIR RULES AND BLOW THEIR WHISTLES IN YOUR EARS

We learn most of our fears from other people. Our parents, our friends, our teachers, people on television and in the movies - they all teach us even when we aren't aware that we are being taught.

People do not generally want to teach us to be afraid. It just happens. We watch someone be afraid of the dark, for example, and that tells us that being afraid of the dark is something that people do to protect themselves. And it does protect us, because a lot of bad things happen in the dark. But it limits us as well because a lot of very nice things also happen in the dark.

Many of the limits we learn do not really make sense. For instance, being cautious about the dark makes sense, but being terrified of the dark does not. Being cautious about talking to strangers makes sense, but being afraid to talk to anyone you don't know does not make sense.

When we can't make sense out of our limits and we refuse to commit them to memory, then those who are trying to impose those limits on us turn to fear to make us believers. As a form of motivation fear works wonders. Few of us will do what we are afraid of doing and in this way our limits become part of our lives.

"I want to wear my red dress to school," the little girl says to her mom.

"Oh no dear," says mom, "you can't wear a red dress. You don't want people laughing at you, do you?"

There was no real reason why the little girl could not wear her red dress to school, except that her mother did not want her to. Because her mother had no rational logic for putting limits on her daughter's wishes, she was forced to turn to the time tested method of parent control, namely 'fear of humiliation, fear of shame, fear of guilt, and fear of anger'.

By the time this mother is finished the child will have many limits acting inside her, and each limit will act just like a referee to keep her playing life by the rules.

I clearly remember the day I first discovered that each of us carries our own group of Refs inside of us. I remember feeling as if I had suddenly understood something really important, something which had the power to make my life a lot easier to live.

I was watching a girls' basketball game at the time. It was junior high school level and the girls were breaking a lot of rules. The referees were continuously calling fouls and blowing their whistles. It was obvious that the girls were becoming increasingly frustrated.

When one girl was called out because of fouls she lost control and started yelling at the referees, stamping her feet in a kind of temper tantrum. She had to be restrained by some of her teammates and by her coach.

As I watched her sit on the bench, angry, frustrated, really wanting to play but now unable to because the refs had decided she had broken the rules, I understood why it was often so hard for me to do some of the things that I wanted to do.

Each one of us learns a personal set of limitations which we carry around inside of us. These limitations become a set of dos and don'ts which combine into a set of rules to live by. These rules work inside of our heads and hearts in the same way that referees work in a game.

Just like referees our internal Refs blow their whistles and make calls according to the limits and rules we have learned to believe are the game rules. The game in this case are the things that we do day by day. And just like real referees our internal Refs call penalties when we break the rules.

LIMIT	**REF WHISTLE**
I can't do that.	feel hopeless
I can't talk to people.	feel inadequate
Life is supposed to be hard.	feel no control

Our internal Refs don't really care what we think about their calls. The rules are the rules and they are meant to be obeyed even if it frustrates us, makes us angry, makes us shake, or even forces us to withdraw from the game to sit and stew on the bench.

Do you remember the first time you tried to jump off a high diving board, and you felt so afraid that you decided not to jump after all? That feeling of unease was a Ref blowing a whistle as it followed a rule meant to protect you. You really didn't want its help, but the Ref blew the whistle anyway. You had reached a limit and the rule said stop.

Have you ever got up to speak in front of a group of people and suddenly your mouth became bone dry and your heart rate increased so fast you thought it was going to jump out of your chest, and when you opened your mouth you found you couldn't speak? Those feelings were your Refs blowing their whistles to keep you from possibly embarrassing yourself.

Have you ever tried to change a bad habit and found that your own body and mind were fighting against you and trying to keep the habit around? That was your Refs blowing their whistles to stop you from going through the anxiety of change.

Your Refs are really trying to protect you. The Ref blowing the whistle on the diving board did not want you to take a chance of hurting yourself when you dove. The Ref that speeds up your heart so much that you find it difficult to move is really trying to protect you from making a fool of yourself in front of others.

Our internal Refs are our fears. The more fears we have the more Refs we carry with us. Together they determine what is possible, what isn't possible, what is legal and what is illegal.

When I first began to make a list of fears which set limits on life I had only four: FOR, FOE, FOF, and FOS. This stood for Fear of Risk, Fear of Embarrassment, Fear of Failure, and Fear of Success. 'Refs' is an acronym formed by taking the first letter of each of those fears: Risk, Embarrassment, Failure, Success.

Now, those four fears making up the first set of Refs are scary enough, but I soon found there were more than four blowing their whistles in us. Some of the fears I hadn't counted were:

MORE FEARS

- Fear of Rejection
- Fear of Fear
- Fear of Feeling
- Fear of Punishment
- Fear of Work
- Fear of Change
- Fear of Loss
- Fear of Pain
- Fear of Intimidation
- Fear of Authority
- Fear of Loss of Control
- Fear of Death

With all those fears blowing whistles and dropping flags and imposing penalties it becomes easy to understand just why our lives are so complicated, and why it is so easy for us to be afraid. We live in the midst of a minefield of fears. Every step we take could activate a fear. Barriers are all around us.

When you realize that the Refs exist, when you realize that we are confined by limits which are kept in place by fears, then we have an opportunity to give ourselves permission to break through our barriers, permission to place more trust in our own abilities and our own desires.

Taking a look at some of the Refs can help us understand them better and give us more control over how they make us act. The Ref that tries to keep us from taking a risk is a particularly powerful fear. When we take a risk we step out of a well worn path and leave ourselves open to making a mistake or failing. The risk Ref wants to keep us on the same path we have always walked and already know is safe.

Failure is another major Ref. Unless it results in physical injury to yourself or to others, there is nothing wrong with failure. In fact, the only time we really learn is when we take risks. When we don't fail we don't learn. It's the Refs who think risk is bad, not life.

The success Ref can prevent us from accomplishing a lot of goals. This sounds a little strange until you stop to think about it a little. Many people walk around thinking they are failures and not knowing what it feels like to be a success. To become successful would cause these people a lot of stress because the way they saw the world would have to change and their minds would have to change. So the Refs blow the whistle every time success is near and the game is called. Being successful is living proof that you are special, and many people simply cannot handle that belief.

If you carry a poor self-image around in your mental wallet you are probably letting your Refs stop you from taking better pictures of who you are. A bad self-image picture can act like a real ball and chain around your ankle and hold you back from doing many of the things which would otherwise make you happy.

You don't have to live by fearing punishment so much that you will refuse to try out new ways of doing things and new ways of feeling and new ways of thinking. Punishment is part of our human way of life. For people who deliberately break the rules and the laws we live by the fear of punishment is a good thing. But for most of us fear of punishment should not be a real concern.

Sure, there are consequences for the things we do. Sometimes you will get yelled at when you make a mistake or when things go wrong. But you don't have to live your life worrying about someone being angry at you. When it does happen you don't have to let a Ref tell you that it hurts enough to stop the game or give you a penalty.

We all experience pain in different ways. For some of us the mere thought of pain is enough to make us afraid, and so a Ref will blow the whistle when pain looks even barely possible. For others pain is more something that can be controlled to some extent.

The more you believe that pain is fearful, the more you will have a Ref blowing a whistle. People who respect pain, but who are not particularly afraid of it, do not have Ref whistles blowing continuously in their mental ears.

Fear of authority is another one of our internal Refs. We tend to fear authority because people with authority, like mom or dad or the boss, usually are bigger and more powerful and control a lot of the things we need. People with authority can take away their love from us. Or they can take away their protection. Or they can punish us. Or they can fire us.

But just because someone has authority over you does not make them better than you, or more special than you, or more important than you. It is critical you believe that. No matter what you have been taught by well meaning parents, or your teachers, or the people you work for, or your friends - it is important to realize that even though limits were placed on us for our own protection, this does not make those limits right.

You have the power to change the things you fear. You have the power to change the rules your Refs blow their whistles by.

Fear is a really good way of getting our attention and warning us that possible danger exists. Fear was not meant to rule our lives. Fear is information.

It is important you understand that the Refs like things the way they are. They like the games you play, they like the penalties that are imposed, and that is why your Refs want to blow their whistles when change threatens. They don't want change coming in and upsetting things. Stability is important in our lives, but too much is deadening.

For some reason which is hard to understand people are afraid to change. Fear of change is probably the greatest single barrier to human communication. Fear of change is more responsible than any other fear for keeping the Refs blowing their whistles regularly.

To change your Refs you have to understand why your Refs blow their whistles as they do. You have to understand what the Refs are trying to protect you from and what limits your Refs want to keep you inside.

And then you have to tell your Refs that you want to change the rules. You have to give yourself permission to change the rules. You have to trust yourself to get along in life by listening to the Refs without always obeying their whistles.

When you do this your Refs will lose a lot of their power to keep you in line. After a while you won't hear their whistles nearly as often. After a while the penalty box will be empty a lot more than it is now.

Chapter 15

WE ARE ALL EXPERTS IN CONSTRUCTING WALLS

Great roads
The Romans built
That men might meet
Yet walls also
To keep men apart
And secure

New centuries
Are gone
And in defeat
The walls are fallen
But the roads endure

Evelyn Hartwich

If we had a choice between building walls and building roads, I think the vast majority of us would choose to build walls. It just seems easier to build walls than it does to build roads.

Roads just seem to be there. We don't remember how much trouble they were to build. We don't notice just how much they control the directions we take. They make travelling a lot easier but we don't realize how important they are until they aren't around and travelling becomes difficult.

Walls, on the other hand, look more difficult than roads, they look more solid. Walls are meant to block, they are meant to separate, to isolate. Roads are meant to join things together, to overcome, to make things easier.

Have you ever thought about walls? Most people don't think about them unless they happen to run into one.

Walls are hard, and they are meant to keep some things in, to separate other things, and to keep some things out. They are flexible in that they can be built from virtually any kind of material, and they work well enough that they can stop almost anything from moving.

We don't seem to think about roads much either. We use them without a great deal of thought, or we wish we had more, but few people give serious thought about building them.

If we do stop to give it some thought we might soon come to the conclusion that roads are ultimately more important than walls.

Walls help us survive, but roads help us grow. Walls keep us safe, but roads allow us to take a risk. Walls help us know what is going on, but roads confront us with new ideas and new problems and new ways of growth. Walls keep us comfortable, but roads keep us going.

Of course, the kind of walls we are talking about really don't have anything to do with bricks or concrete or mortar. The walls we are talking about are made from stuff in the mind like fear, and stubbornness, depression, blaming, avoidance, and nervousness. The walls we are talking about are constructions in our heads which try to stop us from doing things we want to do, or even to stop us from wanting things.

We all have these internal walls. You can't go through life without constructing a maze of walls in your head. But just because they are natural doesn't mean they are necessary, or that you have to build a lot more of them.

When you construct a wall, you make yourself feel as if you are safer. And just like real walls which can be constructed out of almost anything, you can construct mental walls out of hundreds of different materials.

You can use fear as a wall. When you are afraid of something you won't usually go near it. And so it doesn't have much chance of hurting you.

You can refuse to change. You can be stubborn and stay as you are and resist any attempts to improve. When you refuse to believe that change is important you build a really big and powerful wall around yourself.

You can construct a wall around your feeling of self-importance and simply go through life not believing that you are worth much. You don't have to believe you are important. You can wall that feeling out, if you wish.

You can build walls by avoiding the truth, avoiding responsibilities, and avoiding anything that you simply do not want to hear.

You can build walls by blaming other people for all your problems. This is a particularly lovely wall to keep out the necessity for change. When you blame others, it is always someone else's fault, never your fault, and this leaves you feeling as if you are doing what is necessary to survive.

You can build a wall by feeling sorry for yourself, or feeling as if you are all alone. This will allow you to feel that you don't have as much chance for success as other people, and so you can give up easier. If no one loves you, then what is the point in doing anything to improve yourself or what you are doing?

WALL BUILDING INSTRUCTIONS

1. You can use fear as a wall.
2. You can refuse to change.
3. You can feel you are not important.
4. You can believe you are not worth much.
5. You can avoid the truth.
6. You can avoid responsibilities.
7. You can blame other people for all your problems.
8. You can feel sorry for yourself.
9. You can feel all alone.

The object of mental walls is to protect yourself and keep yourself just the way you are. But walls don't work because the real way to protect ourselves is to build roads, something which walls simply will not allow us to do. If you get out from behind your walls you give yourself the opportunity of learning why the walls aren't really necessary.

As long as you are hiding behind a wall, what you could learn from what rests on the other side will forever remain a mystery.

Chapter 16

YOU ARE NOT A PRISONER OF YOUR FROZEN HISTORY

If you take all the things you know, even the things that you don't remember you know, and you add them all up, you will eventually get some idea of who you are.

You are what you know.

You are not what you do not know.

Sometimes people get mixed up with these two ideas. Sometimes people want to be something very much, and so they pretend really hard to be that something, but they are not that something, and in the end they hurt themselves.

If you want to be a ballet dancer, but you never bother to learn ballet, then no matter how many dreams you have in your head about being a dancer you will never succeed.

This works the same way with being a hockey player, a good student, a piano player, a successful worker, a singer, an artist, anything at all you want to be.

You have the potential to be more than you are, but right at this moment, right at this very instant, you are a collection of all the things that have ever happened to you which you carry along inside of you.

Everything you do becomes a part of you. The time you won the game and everybody cheered. The time you lost the game and everybody booed.

The time your friends laughed at you. The time you weren't picked for the team. The time you thought you looked foolish. The time you felt your friends were betraying you. The time someone told you that they loved you. The time you got lost in the woods. The time you felt something in life change, and it scared you because you knew that it had changed forever.

Everything you do becomes part of your history.

You won't remember most of the things that have happened to you. But those things did happen to you, nevertheless, and each one of them has changed you in some way, made you bigger, or made you smaller, or built a wall, or formed a Ref, or made you stronger.

Each new problem you have, and each new solution, and each new action is added to your history until it all adds up and amounts to who you are right at this very moment.

Right now, right at this very instant, you are your history. What you are now is a result of what you were in the past. We can only be what we know, and what we know doesn't change as easily as we think it does. In fact, we actually resist change. We seem to need a really good reason before we will let change happen to alter our beliefs.

It is not only our history that is frozen. Our history forms our belief system. Our beliefs determine what we will learn and how well we will learn. Since we can only think about what we know about, that means that our history determines what goes on inside our minds.

All this really makes sense. If you have known a lot of love from your family it will be a lot easier to think in terms of love when problems with other people come along. When you have known a lot of love thoughts from others, it is really a lot easier to think about love thoughts for others.

Our history makes things familiar to us. If you have known a lot of success in your past you will be prepared to recognize success when it comes to you again. People tend to be more comfortable with things that are familiar. It is because of this that our history makes us feel good or bad about what we know.

All this is great, of course, if you are satisfied with your history and how you turned out. This is great if you like who you are. Because your history is frozen, and you resist change, you will continue to be 'who you are' later on this afternoon, this evening, tomorrow, and every tomorrow after that until something dramatic happens and you change your history.

But what do you do if you do not like who you are? What happens if your history adds up to create a person who you do not particularly like? What do you do then?

Since we resist change, even when we want some kind of change to happen, we tend not to change. We tend to be the same person we are for a very long time.

Many people will tell you that we are prisoners of our history. But you don't have to be. If you are the sum story of what you know, and you want to change who you are, then you can change what you know.

Change what you believe and you change what you know. When you change what you believe you change the entire world around you. This might sound too simple to be true. But that is because you find it hard to believe that change is easy.

If you believe that change is easy, and if someone takes the time to show you how easy it really is, then change becomes the most natural and the healthiest thing in the world.

Suppose you are worried about a test. The only reason you are worried is because of things you know, or don't know. You may know that you don't remember the facts needed for the test. Or you may know that you didn't study enough for the test. Or you may even know that you never do well on tests. These are things you know and remember which end up causing you to worry.

If you want to change the way you worry about tests, then you have to change what you know about tests. That is really simple. By doing this you will have changed, because as soon as you learn to believe something new you have changed your history.

You could study harder to come to know more facts. This would give you more confidence. Or you could change what you believe about tests, about how important they are, about what they mean to you, about what they really mean to your life.

When you change what you know about something you begin to change what you believe about that something, and this changes the way you think about it. This helps you change the way you feel, and this helps change the way you act.

You are not a prisoner of your past. You are the director of your present. You can choose what you know, if you want to, and if you believe you can.

Chapter 17

ANGER IS NORMAL BUT THAT DOESN'T MAKE IT RIGHT

Anger seems to be something that is natural. If we look hard enough we can find it everywhere. We can find it in books, we can find anger in our friends, we can find it in our employers, in our teachers, in our parents, in the movies, on the streets, even in ourselves.

Anger is a basic part of our lives. Yet we really don't talk about it much. We seem to be a little afraid of anger. It is something we want to hide out of sight, and when it does come up we want to deal with it quickly so that it can be pushed back out of sight again.

Feelings of anger are normal. We may not like it but anger is part of what makes us human. Feeling guilty about feeling angry is as pointless as feeling guilty about growing hair on your legs.

Anger happens regardless of how we feel. Everyone feels that way once in a while. Since it is going to happen whether we like it or not we need to learn how to control it so that it is unable control us.

We are born with the ability to get angry built right into our brains. When there is a large difference between what we want and what we get one of the most natural things for us to do seems to involve getting angry. It is this anger that often motivates us to close the gap.

There is something in anger which helps us focus on what we do not like. When we get angry we get stronger for a few moments. This is a tremendous help for survival. The problem comes when we think we need to be that little bit stronger all the time, and we use anger as our main way of dealing with life.

Can you imagine being filled with anger all the time? Can you imagine having angry thoughts constantly in your mind? Can you imagine the kind of stress and anxiety your body would have to put up with if you used anger as a focus for dealing with your all of your problems?

You would find it impossible to relax. You would be jumpy, constantly on edge, ready to fly off the handle. And of course, you would be constantly looking for someone to be angry at, because what's the use of being angry unless someone sees it?

I guess if no one but you is around to be angry at you might actually have to resort to being angry at yourself all the time. There are actually people like that around. You can see it in the way they stand, ready for a fight, ready to lash out.

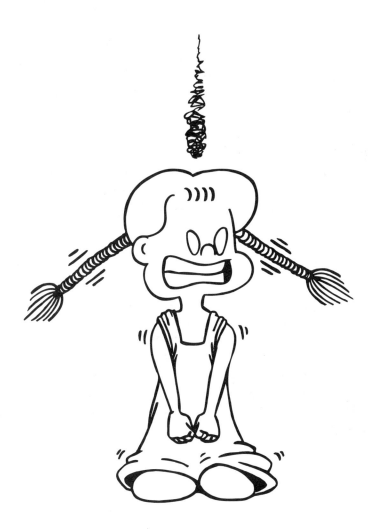

Even though it seems like a rotten way to live, anger does have certain benefits. A lot of times anger works. A lot of times a sudden surge of anger will get you what you want.

If someone does something you don't like, and you get angry, they get the message immediately. You don't have to say a great deal because your anger says it all. Very often your anger will upset people so much they will do what you want them to do.

Of course, what you can use on people, other people can use on you. People use anger all the time to try to control you. They may not understand what they are doing but that doesn't diminish the results they obtain.

Anger has two main messages. One is that violence is just around the corner unless something happens to stop the anger. The other message is that I will reject you if you do not listen to the warning. When I see you get angry, and I become afraid as a result, then I am far more likely to behave in a way which will please you.

When dogs and bears get angry they make noises in their throats and bare their teeth and raise their hackles. When people get angry their eyes flare, their bodies pump up and grow tense, they stick out their jaws, and they seem more than ready to launch themselves into a fight. It is easy to recognize a person being angry. You don't need a lot of schooling to recognize anger as a warning.

Anger is used by a lot of people in a lot of different ways. It is an amazingly flexible tool. When we aren't aware of how it works it can cause a lot of confusion.

Bullies use anger as a part of their overall method of trying to dominate you. Others may use anger to show that their feelings are hurt. Others may use anger to show their hatred. Others may use anger to make them feel stronger and more defiant. Still others may use anger to make people worry and feel anxious or afraid.

Parents may use anger to show their children that they mean business. Teachers may use anger to control their students. Friends may use anger to show their displeasure. Married couples may use anger to punish their partners.

While anger might work temporarily to manipulate others, it doesn't work for long. You may be able to use anger to get your way now but eventually that anger will backfire and it will actually prevent you from getting what you want. Eventually the fear that your anger causes in others will either fade away or it will cause a backlash against you.

If I aim my anger at you for long enough, eventually you will rebel against me. You might choose to stay around and seek revenge. You might choose to challenge my anger with your anger. You should realize, however, that seldom are the feelings of resentment, or the desire to get even, very positive or productive. Long term anger is damaging to the health of both mind and body.

Anger fails in another respect as well. When you are angry, you simply cannot think very well. When you are angry you don't have control over what you are doing, how you are feeling, or your thoughts. In nearly any encounter when two people are negotiating the person who stays in control the best usually wins the most.

Anger can be useful as a temporary tool to get us going. For example, we could get angry because we failed a test, and this could provide the motivation for forcing us to study harder to pass the next test. But anger over the long term hurts us far more than it helps. It makes everything too black and white, and does not leave room for compromise.

The bottom line of anger is simple. We are all born with the natural ability to get angry. How we get angry, how often we get angry, or what makes us angry are all choices we make.

We are all born with the ability to play the bagpipes, but only a few of us will ever choose to learn how to play. In the same way we are all born with the ability to get angry and how we choose to use it is up to us.

If we use anger as a focus for getting along in life then we are really allowing anger to run our lives for us. Anger should be used to help us live, not to run the way we live.

A PLAN
FOR STEERING YOURSELF
IN THE RIGHT
DIRECTION

Chapter 18

YOU KAN'T LOSE UNLESS YOU THINK YOU KAN

'K' stands for knowledge, 'A' stands for action, and 'N' stands for the nervous system which makes up your brain. Put them together and you KAN do almost anything in this world that you put your mind to. Put your knowledge together with your actions and the power of your brain and you have all the tools you will ever need to be the best you KAN possibly be.

The apostrophe in KAN'T stands for a 'negative' or 'take away' belief. The 'T' stands for all the 'thoughts' that you have. Place the negative in front of your thoughts, and what you arrive at are the negative thoughts that prevent you from acting in positive ways.

This is one of the most important motivational tools any person KAN learn how to use. When you 'know' you KAN do things, you KAN'T lose.

You lose only when you stop trying, when you stop believing you KAN. You lose when you send the message to your brain to give up. You lose when you admit that you KAN'T. When you KAN'T you know that your actions negate your thoughts.

It may sound strange, but it really isn't. When you know you KAN'T, then you probably KAN'T.

When you know you KAN, and you believe you KAN, and you are persistent enough to keep trying, and you use problem solving, and you deliberately make the right choices, then eventually you will obtain what you wish.

You may not obtain exactly what you wish. You may obtain only part of it. But you will obtain what is reasonable considering how hard you tried, and how possible it is to obtain what you want.

That is life.

By looking for the best in what comes to you, you are looking for opportunities rather than looking for defeats and failures. And anyone who looks for opportunities more than they look for failures will meet more successes than defeats.

That is mathematical.

Suppose you had a coin and you wanted to flip a tail, and suppose you flipped it once and it came up a head. Would you have failed?

No. You just have not succeeded that particular time. Even if you flip again and it comes up head again, you still have not failed. Eventually, if you flip that coin again, and even again, you will flip a tail.

A tail is inevitable. That is life. That is mathematical.

The only time you will fail is when you stop flipping, when you admit you are unable to flip a tail, and when you believe that further action is pointless, and so you walk away.

Believing you KAN is the first step in achieving your dreams.

But how about the boy who strikes out each time he steps up to bat? Should he put all his hopes and dreams into being a player in the big league some day? Can he achieve his dream? Should he give up his other dreams and concentrate completely on playing baseball?

Probably not. Even our dreams should contain some logic. It is pointless trying to be a professional basketball player when you were born really short.

There are some things which you will simply not be able to do. There is no point in dreaming of being a fish and swimming underwater without breathing apparatus if you were born a human being. There is no point in dreaming of writing a great novel if you can't read or write and you aren't really interested in learning.

But you KAN achieve dreams that make sense. The boy could continue to play baseball and continue to try hitting the ball and one day he will probably find that hitting the ball is getting easier and easier. He may never be big league, but this shouldn't stop him from playing a game he enjoys.

And you KAN swim like a fish if you use scuba tanks. You KAN write a great novel, even if you KAN'T read or write, by telling your story into a tape recorder and hiring someone else to type it.

Anything is possible to some degree if you continually send 'I KAN' messages to your brain, if you are focused, and if you believe you KAN.

A PLAN
FOR STEERING YOURSELF
IN THE RIGHT
DIRECTION

Chapter 19

YOUR AUTOMATIC PILOT WORKS WITHOUT A WHOLE LOT OF THINKING

Have you ever stopped to wonder what habits are all about? Not many people do.

Habits are really not good or bad - they are simply behaviors we do over and over. We can think in ways that are habits, we can act in ways that are habits, we can say things in ways that are habits, and we can even feel in ways that are habits.

We tend to concentrate on habits only when we don't like them or want to get rid of them. Those habits that do help us, the ones that help keep us going by taking care of the routine stuff, don't get much attention at all.

Try living without habits, even for a short period of time, and you will soon see just how important they are to us. Without habits life would be really complicated.

The kinds of movies you like, the kinds of food you like and don't like, the kinds of books you enjoy reading, the way you walk, the way you talk, the things you like to talk about, the way you move your head, the way you solve problems, the kinds of people you like, even the thoughts you have: these are all determined by your habits.

A habit is something you do which doesn't require a great deal of thinking. If you had to take the time to think about your likes and dislikes before you acted, you would spend most of your day trying to figure out what you were going to do next, and you would not get much done.

But what does it mean when we say that a habit does not need a whole lot of thinking? How can you do anything without thinking about it? If we don't think about what we are doing, then how do we manage to get anything done? Isn't thinking part of everything we do? If we do things without thinking, are we still responsible for what we do?

There have been a lot of theories trying to explain how habits work. Because we are dealing with parts of the mind that are invisible it is a good idea to remember that these explanations are really only stories made up to try and make sense of what can't be seen. The better the story sounds, the more we believe it, but that does not prevent the whole thing from being just a story.

Making stories up is not unusual. We do it a lot, and because we believe the stories, they really help us. For example, there used to be a story that the sun revolved around the earth. That made all of us feel more important because it put us at the center of everything. But even though the story made us feel good it wasn't true because the earth does revolve around the sun no matter how it makes us feel.

There used to be a story that the earth was flat, and that if we sailed too close to the edge we would fall right off. That story made sailors very careful when they sailed, but it also made them feel better because they believed they knew what was happening and this made them feel more in command.

That is what stories are really for. They help us believe that we really know what is happening, and this helps us feel as if we really are in control of things. We really aren't, but it makes us feel better if we believe we are.

I want to tell you a story that I made up. It is a story that I use to help me make some kind of sense out of what goes on in my head. It works well for me. It helps me understand where habits come from, and why they are so hard to break, and what I can do to change what I don't like. As a result I don't feel so frustrated and anxious when a habit refuses to change or go away.

The main characters in this story are you, and a car.

Often when we compare one thing we don't understand to something that we do understand we come to know the unknown thing a little better.

With that in mind my story begins by comparing the way your mind and body work to the way a car works. Even if your mind and body do not work like a car, (and they really don't), it does help to get a better picture about what is going on in our heads.

The following chart will help you get a good idea about what the comparison looks like.

CAR PART	**MENTAL PART**
1. Engine	Motivation
2. Performance	Feelings
3. Tires & Movement	Actions
4. Steering	Beliefs
5. Luggage	Knowledge & Memory
6. Road maps	Goals
7. Gas	Thoughts
8. Driver	Automatic pilot

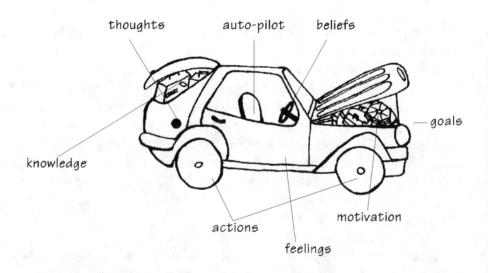

The nice thing about this story is that it is simple:

1. Your motivation moves you along just like an engine moves a car along. The bigger your engine, the bigger your motivation, the better you move along.

2. How well your engine performs, how fast it goes, depends on how you feel. If you feel good or positive, the engine goes really smoothly and works really well. But if you feel bad or negative, the engine just does not perform as well. It might go fast, but it will go too fast, without a lot of control.

3. & 4. Your beliefs tell you how to steer, and how you steer is how you act. If you believe you should drive in the passing lane, then you will act by steering the car in that direction, and the wheels will turn in that direction, and the car will move in that direction.

    If you believe that you KAN play the piano you will steer yourself in that direction by acting to find a piano, and taking lessons, and actually sitting down to learn how to play the piano. If you believe you won't ever be able to play the piano, you will steer yourself right away from the whole subject area.

5. You carry your luggage in the trunk just as you carry your memories and knowledge in your mind. Your luggage is your history, your habits, the things you know. A car cannot go anywhere without its trunk, and neither can you.

6. You follow maps in your car in order to get to where you want to go. You use your goals to guide you from place to place and problem to problem in life. The roads you take are the solutions you use to solve your problems.

7. Gasoline generates the power to move your car and keeps the engine running, and your thoughts do the same job for your mental motor. When you stop thinking, you either let your habits tell you where to go, or you stop moving forward.

We now come to #8, the last part of the story. A car is controlled by a driver who sits behind the wheel, steers, puts a foot on the gas or on the brake, and generally directs the way things happen.

Your mental car is a little more complicated. Most of the time you don't really do the driving. Most of the time you sit in your seat and watch. Most of the time your automatic pilot does all the actual driving work.

And what do you do? Most of the time you ride shotgun on your automatic pilot. You check things out. You look for problems. You watch for other cars on the road. You look for bad roads or for roadblocks, and you tell your automatic pilot what is happening.

Maybe an easier image to help you understand would be to imagine that you are an executive riding in the back of a stretch limousine and saying, "Home James," to your automatic pilot. While you sit back and take care of other business your automatic pilot drives you home. That is what habits do for you. They allow you to sit in the passenger seat while your internal chauffeur drives you where you want to go.

You can see a good example of your automatic pilot in operation when you ride your bicycle. When you climb on your bike and ride off down the street, how often do you actually stop and think about how you should hold the handle bars, or how you should hold your body to maintain balance, or how hard you should push your feet against the pedals to go the speed you want? Unless something happens to focus your attention on these things, most frequently your automatic pilot takes over and makes everything happen.

What do you do while your automatic pilot is making it possible to ride the bicycle? You do the watching, you look for trouble, and you decide where you want to go and how fast you want to get there, you monitor yourself to see how tired you are getting.

And how does this automatic pilot know what to do? Quite simply, your habits tell it what to do.

Most of the things you do you have done many times before. You have sat down thousands of times before. You have picked up a spoon or a fork thousands of times before. You have dried yourself off with a towel thousands of times before. Your automatic pilot has the memory of all these things stored (remember the car trunk?). It knows when you usually do things, and how you usually do things, and then when those things need to be done again, it does what you usually do.

Your automatic pilot moves fast, moves slow, moves recklessly, moves safely, is afraid to take a risk, wants to be dependent, meets situations with anger, loves to think, hates to think, is full of fear, wants to veg out in front of the television, is courageous - it does exactly what its habits tell it to do.

All this is terrific. It frees you to use your mind to be creative, to solve problems, to gather information.

There is a difficulty, however. Your automatic pilot finds it very hard to change. It will follow the learning path and change slowly over time, but you already know from your own life just how difficult it is to change a habit.

Your automatic pilot will change, but only if you provide lots of proof that you need to change, or if you can fool it into changing, or if you have the strength to change it.

In general, once the automatic pilot has learned to do something, it wants to continue doing it that way forever and will resist change.

Much of the time this resistance is good. If change was easy your automatic pilot wouldn't have the knowledge and expertise to work as well as it has to. By resisting, your automatic pilot gives you a chance to learn all the stuff you need to know in order to survive and be effective.

The problem arises when the automatic pilot becomes so accustomed to acting in a certain way that it continues to act in that way even though you know what it is doing doesn't work.

For instance, maybe you have learned that the best way to handle a friend with hurt feelings is simply to ignore what you have done. Because it seems to work with one friend, you use the same method to deal with the hurt feelings of other friends. Unfortunately this method doesn't work with your other friends. Their feelings stay hurt, but you have a lot of difficulty changing your habits so you continue acting in the same way in spite of the problems this creates in your life.

The fantastic part of this story is that you can change the way the pilot operates. You can take over control of the car and deliberately change the way you feel, change the way you act, change what you know, and change what you think.

You can change the choices you make. If you do this for long enough eventually you will remove the old habit program from the driver's seat, and install a new habit in the driver's program.

CHANGING THE AUTOMATIC PILOT

1. It will change if it finds change pleasurable.
2. It will change if something really dramatic happens to you, for instance if you fall off your bike, or get kicked by a horse, or get fired from your job.
3. It will change slowly over a long period of time without being aware that it is really changing.
4. It will change if it is forced to repeat something many times over a long period.

A few minutes every morning, and a few minutes at night spent in changing your choices, changing your feelings, actions, knowledge and thinking, and within the very short span of thirty days you will have taught your automatic pilot a new way of driving.

For really big problems, when life is severely broken, it may take longer than thirty days. There is nothing magic about thirty days. Thirty days just happens to be the most common chunk of time that is required to change your automatic pilot.

Once the new habit has been installed, the automatic pilot will take over again and you can continue being the passenger. It is fantastic the way it works. And you do it all simply by controlling and changing your choices.

So, is the story real? Probably not. Is the comparison between a car and your mind a real one? Probably not. Do we really have an automatic pilot in our heads? Probably not.

What is important is not the story. What is important is not the fantasy that some automatic pilot drives you through life. What is important is that your belief system allows you to change your habits any time you wish. What is important is that your beliefs allow you to control the things you do, and how you do them.

We are responsible for what we do. Thoughts are labels that we stick onto life to give it some meaning for us. Habits join thoughts and actions together in ways which work so well for us that we keep them around by storing them as patterns for our automatic pilot to follow. This is how we steer ourselves through life. This is how we are responsible for our habits.

A PLAN
FOR STEERING YOURSELF
IN THE RIGHT
DIRECTION

Chapter 20

FAILURE IS ONLY A STATE OF MIND

How do you feel when you fail? Rotten? Worried? Like you haven't measured up? Like the world is going to fall in on you? Like people who don't make mistakes are better than you? Like you shouldn't be proud of yourself any longer?

The way we use it in our day to day life failure is not a pretty word. It is a hurting word. It is not a word to make us feel more powerful. It is a word which tends to make us question our own value, and our own worth.

But why? Who said that failure is bad? Why is it considered so harmful? It is a major and necessary part of life. We fail in things every day. So why are we so hard on ourselves when we do?

There are a lot of theories which try to explain what failure is and it is hard to find one explanation which really makes sense.

Failure is not a reflection of who you are. If you don't get an 'A' on a test, that doesn't mean that you are less valuable than someone who does manage to get an 'A'.

Failure is information. That is all it is. It tells us that what happened was not entirely successful according to what we wanted to happen.

As information, failure generally does not hurt. Normally, it is not what we do wrong that hurts, but how we feel about what we did. We take failure information, and we attach a big negative value judgment onto it, and all of a sudden it becomes something really major. All of a sudden failure becomes a reflection of our lack of worth.

Failure is the result of certain thoughts, actions, feelings, and knowledge being applied to a problem, with the results not turning out the way we wanted. We say, "that is wrong," or "that feels terrible," or "no one will see that as important," and that is the message we give ourselves.

Failure is a judgment we make based upon how well we feel we have done. So is success. Success is also a judgment. The only difference is that success tells us what works, while mistakes tell us what doesn't work.

Both success and failure change your life. Success does not guarantee that the change will be good for you, nor does failure guarantee that it will be bad.

For instance, you could spend months trying to grow a plant from an unidentified seed, and finally succeed only to find that you have grown broccoli, a vegetable you really don't like very much, and because you grew it you find it on your plate for supper. You win, but you also lose.

It is really important to understand that you will never receive any success without a string of failures. No one has ever been successful without failing first, many times.

What you need to do is give yourself permission to fail, give yourself permission to make mistakes, and above all give yourself permission to learn from what you do.

When you do allow yourself to be unsuccessful without making yourself feel bad, you reduce a lot of anxiety because there isn't as much pressure on you to be right all the time, or to be successful all the time.

When you see failures and mistakes as sources of information about what not to do, or about how not to proceed, then you can actually gain in self-confidence from both failure and success.

If we are not prepared to accept our own lack of success, or if our aim is to achieve nothing less than perfection, then failure will be with us always.

I once gave a really good student an 'A' grade on a project. Later, she came to me and wanted to discuss her mark. It seemed that she needed more explanation of the evaluation she had received.

I pointed out that I had already given her an 'A'. She said she appreciated the 'A', but what kind of 'A' was it?

I said it was an 'A' 'A'. She said she appreciated that, but what kind of 'A' 'A' was it? Was it a good 'A' 'A', or just a satisfactory good 'A' 'A'?

I told her it was a really good 'A' 'A'. She said that was great, but was it a really, really good 'A' 'A', or just a really good 'A' 'A'?

About this time it became quite obvious that the young girl would never be satisfied. While she certainly had a definition for failure - which seemed to be almost everything she did that was not perfect and better than everyone in sight - she did not have the same kind of definition for success.

She did not really know what success was, or how to recognize it, or how to accept it. Somehow, in her mind, success eluded her. She could never quite get a grip on it.

When you make your own definition about what you believe failure to be, construct it in a positive fashion. Give yourself room to take risks. Be willing to try your hand at new things. Be willing to accept the possibility of making a fool of yourself in order to learn.

You see, failure generally can't hurt you unless you believe it can. Failure is only really important when it hurts you in a physical way, or hurts other people.

If you fail to get out of the path of a truck and you get hit, that kind of failure can hurt. A lot. If you jump out of an airplane and your parachute fails to open, that kind of failure can hurt. But those kinds of failures do not happen as frequently as we might think. Most of the time our failures are only in our heads.

Failure helps us succeed. That is what it does for us. It helps us know what works and what doesn't work. It helps us learn. It is not meant to make us feel bad, or to feel like we are nothing. Success is built upon a solid foundation of failures.

Give yourself permission to fail, and you will also be giving yourself permission to succeed.

Chapter 21

TALK IT OVER WITH YOURSELF

I can still remember the day I learned that I was not the only person in the world to carry on conversations in my head.

I don't know when or how I learned that mental conversations were not supposed to be a good thing. I guess I heard adults make fun of people on the street who were talking to themselves. People who heard voices were thought to be a little odd. I guess I put it all together and came up with the belief that it was a little strange to have internal chats with myself.

Because no one ever talked to me about it, and because I had never learned anything about it in school, I spent a few of my younger years feeling just a little uncomfortable about the whole thing.

When I say that I talk to myself , I mean that one part of me says something in my head and then some other part of me replies with something else. One part might say, "I think I want to go to sleep," and another part might say, "Its too early to go to bed, let's party."

Your brain uses this self-talk as a major part of learning and it happens non-stop. It is a major tool for understanding what is going on around you. Your mind is never silent. We have 50,000 thoughts a day, each day and every day. We are continuously analyzing, searching, probing, judging, and evaluating through self-talk.

Rather than try to get rid of our self-talk voices because we are afraid of them, or because we think there is something wrong with them, we should realize how much they do for us and learn how to use them.

Self-talk provides us with massive amounts of information. When we argue with ourselves, for example, we generate a lot more alternatives.

"Do this," one voice says, while another argues, "Don't do this". As the debate grows, more information is brought out to support each view, and in this way you get a much better understanding of what is happening.

"Do this because it will help you get a promotion," one voice says. "But I don't really want a promotion, I would rather do something else," another voice continues. If you begin to analyze what the voices say, you can soon uncover information you may not have known before.

Self-talk only works if you listen. It only works if you pay attention to what you are telling yourself. If you don't listen, or if you try to turn the voices off, or if you try to run away from them, you will learn nothing.

Some people find it difficult to deal with their self-talk. As a result, they get nervous, or they get stressed, or they get anxious. The more upset and uptight they get the higher their stress level grows and the more difficult it is for them to be effective.

Your voices can act like an early warning system. When they tell you to be cautious, or when they warn you of possible danger, you are preparing yourself and making yourself aware that something harmful might happen to you. You don't have to listen to those warnings, but you would be really wise to take them into account.

And when the voices make guesses, or when they explain how you feel inside, they are often translating your language of feeling into your verbal language, and trying to tell you in words just how you feel. Once again, however, you need to take the time to listen. You can't reject what you hear just because you don't like what you hear.

Your voices can act like a pep rally for those times when you are feeling uncertain or feeling down. You can use them to encourage yourself, to give yourself credit, to pump yourself up with enthusiasm.

You can use your self-talk to help you go that extra distance when you find the going getting tough. The extra effort your voices can give you could actually spell the difference between success and failure.

Tell yourself, "You can do it." If you tell yourself over and over again that you can do it you will increase your chances of doing it. Or if you tell yourself that, "My problems are not big enough to stop me," and you tell yourself over and over again, you will be amazed at how much extra energy you will receive.

Try it the next time you feel down or low. Tell yourself that you are okay. Talk to yourself about all the positive things you could find when you take the time to look. Tell yourself that you are doing a good job. Talk to yourself about the options that are open to you, about the choices you can make.

Self-talk can also be used negatively. Your voices can be used to resist change, to stop yourself from taking a risk, and to keep yourself from feeling special. We hear "no" far more than we hear "yes" in our lives, and before we are aware of what we are doing we are saying "no" to ourselves.

Your self-talk can often be negative and critical and if you believe what you hear you may often think it is a wise idea to run away and hide. Your voices will often tell you that caution is better than spontaneity, or that going back is better than going forward simply because going forward will cost you more effort.

Your voices often tell you that you can't do what it is that you want to do. They can rob you of your enthusiasm. They can make you afraid, or angry, or even feel empty. When they do this, your voices are quite simply deceiving you.

While we create the world with our beliefs, we do not necessarily create it truthfully. Sometimes our voices help us pretend that something is not happening because we need it not to happen to feel special. We don't want something to be true, so we talk ourselves into believing that it isn't true.

I don't really know how we manage to talk to ourselves, or what the brain does that gives us the ability to carry on conversations in our heads. I only know that we do manage to make our voices sound slightly different when we talk to ourselves and this helps us listen better.

The idea of self-talk might seem unusual, but it really shouldn't. Most writers hear the voices of the characters they are writing about in their minds. If you asked those writers to be honest many would say that the voices almost act by themselves.

It is important you realize that you control your voices. If you don't like what the voices are saying then you can change what they say.

It is important that you believe you have this control otherwise you might feel inclined to sit back and let the voices tell you what to do. Too many people use their voices as excuses for doing nothing. They do not want to accept responsibility for what they do, and so they conveniently blame their voices.

The mind is amazing, whether we want to use it or not.

A PLAN
FOR STEERING YOURSELF
IN THE RIGHT
DIRECTION

Chapter 22

EXPECTING THE WORST DOES NOT RESULT IN GETTING THE BEST

I heard something the other day that brought back a lot of unpleasant thinking habits. A man on the radio was talking about how useless it was to expect the best to happen. He was saying that people who aren't prepared for failure end up failing more often than people who expect failure.

While I do respect the man's right to be negative and to think the worst, I also think he was going out of his way to hurt himself. He even made fun of people who wanted to expect the best. He said we were silly. He said that we should find a way to keep our feet on the ground as if people who expect the best live in a world of make-believe.

I know how the man on the radio feels. There was a time when I was almost afraid to hope for the best. I thought that if I hoped for the best I was really setting myself up for a fall. It seemed to make far more sense to simply expect the worst to happen, and then, when it did happen, I never had to be disappointed.

If I was lucky enough to have the best happen to me then that was a bonus.

But really, when you stop to think about it, isn't that a hopeless way to live? If all you expect is the worst then you can almost be certain that only the worst will happen. After a while you won't even be able to recognize a good thing when it does manage to get through all the negative stuff and happen. You will be so accustomed to the worst that you won't know a good thing when you see it.

That kind of thinking made sense to me at one time, so did worry, guilt and anxiety. It made sense that I should worry about what might or might not happen in the future. And it made sense that I should feel guilt about what had happened in the past. After all, everyone did it, didn't they? And if everyone did it, then it must be natural, right?

There is a story a friend told me that really explains just how wrong I was back then. It seems that there was a girl who did not feel guilty about things in the past. The mistakes she had made and the negative experiences she had lived through were part of her memory, but she did not live in a state of regret about what she had done wrong. She didn't let the things she had failed to do control her life, and she seldom expected the worst to happen.

After listening to her friends, and after reading books and watching movies and television, she finally decided that she must be missing something. Everywhere she looked she found people happily engaged in expecting the worst and feeling the worst. And since everyone was doing it

she thought that maybe feeling guilty and worrying a lot must have a lot of benefits that she was missing.

So she decided that she would go about feeling guilty and expecting the worst. She figured that if she was in good physical condition that she could worry and expect the worst better. To get in better shape she started riding her bike for an hour each day after supper.

She figured she would need more strength to feel guilty really well, so she set about eating healthy meals. She cut out a lot of junk food.

She figured that she would have to be able to think well in order to know what to feel guilty about and what to worry about. To help her thinking, she started doing relaxation exercises to focus her mind better.

She searched through her past for something to feel guilty about, and she got herself ready to expect the worst to happen in the future.

Finally, she got a good night's sleep so that she could get up in the morning and really get a fresh start at worrying and feeling guilty.

The morning came and she started. Afternoon came and passed and soon it got to be evening and she just couldn't make herself feel guilty. She found that it was really difficult to worry for a long period of time.

She ate a good supper and got a good night's sleep and then she got up early the next morning and got to work trying to feel guilty again. Still nothing happened. She tried and tried to worry about something, but the best she could do was to get a little upset for a few minutes. She tried for three whole days before she finally gave up.

This story explains a couple of things to me. First of all, you don't have to feel guilty. You don't have to worry about the things you did in the past. You can live with all the mistakes you have made without regretting any of them. We all make mistakes. So what? We should learn from our mistakes, but we shouldn't live with them for the rest of our lives, and carry them with us like weights tied around our necks.

The story also showed me that if I really want to feel guilty and expect the worst that I should not prepare for it by getting lots of rest, or eating healthy foods, or doing relaxation exercises to get rid of my stress and focus my thinking.

If the girl really wanted to feel bad she should have eaten all kinds of rich foods, stayed up late at night, got no exercise, and looked for things to depress her nervous system.

Too often we confuse worry with doing something constructive. Worry is not problem solving. Nor is expecting the worst very good problem solving. A little worry helps give us information. A little negative expectation gives us information. But once that information has been gathered, worry and negative expectation don't do anything for us. All they do is depress us, slow us down, keep us from trying new things.

Concern is healthy. Worry is unhealthy. Concern helps us analyze problems and think about strategies. Concern helps us make choices, while worry keeps us from making choices by taking away our confidence in the choices we do make.

Worry gets our feelings so worked up that our choices are not clear. Worry gets us so worked up that the only thing we find ourselves really good at is worrying. Worry breeds more worry which breeds more worry.

Some people say that they don't want to worry, but that worry is a habit. I think they are right. Worry is a habit. Guilt is also a habit. Expecting the worst to happen is also a habit. They are all habits which combine to keep us stuck just where we are.

But not worrying about what is going to happen, and not worrying about what has happened, are also habits. We learn not to worry in exactly the same way that we learn to worry. What we can learn, we can also unlearn. That is the absolutely wonderful part about learning and change. It can move us, improve us, and make life better.

You can change the guilt habit into the non-guilt habit. You can change the worry habit into the non-worry habit. And one of the easiest ways of doing this is to never let a negative thought complete itself. Never let a negative action complete itself. Listen to the negative, get information from it, and then simply release it, stop clutching it, let it go.

We are not completely responsible for the thoughts which come into our heads. We are, however, responsible for the thoughts which we keep in our heads. We are not always responsible for the things we do, but we are responsible for the things we keep doing, and the things we do not try to correct.

You have choices. One of the easiest ways to change is to find these choices. Each of us builds life problem by problem, thought by thought, day by day. We build a structure in our heads which tells us what life should be like, and then we use the things we do and think to fill that structure with proof.

Thinking about the best is not silly. In fact, it is really intelligent. Even in the midst of deep unhappiness there are positive things that can be found if we try hard enough to find them. You can be prepared for the worst to happen without carrying around all the negative stuff which is part of the worst.

Positive thoughts are like many things in this world, they are always there, but you have to invite them in or they will stay away, you have to find them or they will stay hidden.

Of course, being positive is not the complete answer. It is only part of the answer. Thinking about the worst, and thinking negatively, are also part of the problem, and in many ways they are the problem.

Chapter 23

FREEDOM IS SOMETHING YOU LEARN

I was talking to a teacher a little while ago and she told me a story that has given me a lot to think about. It wasn't one of the most important stories you might hear. It wasn't terribly dramatic, it didn't involve violence, and no one actually got hurt - and yet there was something about it which makes it important. The story was about a young girl who was caught chewing gum in class.

Chewing gum in class is not really a monstrous crime. It can get stuck under seats and in little girls' pigtails, but that doesn't make it something that police should be called in for, or that parents should be notified about. But chewing gum is nevertheless not allowed in the vast majority of schools and this school was no exception.

When my friend questioned the girl about chewing gum the answer the student gave was really enlightening, and it caused my friend some concern.

The student said that she chewed gum in class because she liked chewing gum. It was as simple as that. That makes sense a little bit, doesn't it? If you like doing something, and if you are a free person, then you should have the right to do something as innocent as chewing gum in class.

That makes sense - or does it?

Chewing gum or not chewing gum really raises the whole question of freedom. If the girl was really free did she have the right to chew gum? If she was free, did the teacher have the right to stop the girl from chewing gum?

Where does freedom begin, and where does freedom end? If you are free do you have the right to make any choice you wish? If you don't have the right to make any choice you wish, does that mean you are no longer free?

In a way, I actually feel sorry for that girl. If she continues to believe that she has the right to do whatever she pleases, when she pleases, and where she pleases, she will almost certainly have a very stressful and anxious life. If that remains her attitude then she will find resistance almost everywhere she turns.

It is not just a matter of chewing gum when she is not supposed to chew gum. It is a matter of understanding that our society requires each and every one of us to have the inner strength to obey certain rules and laws, whether we like them or not. When we all work by the same rules, life becomes less threatening.

When I know that you won't pull out a knife and threaten me just because I did something you don't like, and you know the same thing, then we can both live side by side, even if we don't know each other, and neither one of us will have to worry about our safety. That takes a lot of stress out of life.

Freedom has two sides to it. Freedom gives us rights. It gives us the right to be happy, to live without fear, to make our own choices. But freedom also says that in return for giving us rights we also must accept some responsibilities, we must also do things we do not necessarily want to do.

You have the right to life, but you also have the responsibility to eat in order to keep that life going. There are times when you probably don't want to eat, but if you stop eating long enough you will die.

As an adult, there will be times when you want to run away and live like a hermit and forget all your responsibilities, but that would hurt your family and so you don't run away.

I'm sure that there are times when you would like to stay up all night with your music blasting, but you can't because that would probably disturb a lot of other people.

There are times when you don't want to do your work, but the reality of not being the best you can be, or being criticized for not doing what you are responsible for doing, forces you to do what you don't want to do.

Freedom isn't something that happens only on the outside. Freedom is something that happens inside your heart and head. You can abuse your own rights just as easily as you can abuse the rights of others. You have the right to happiness, but you can override that right by choosing to act in ways which will not bring happiness.

You have the right to self-confidence, but you can deliberately choose not to give yourself permission to value who you are. Strangely, what we find is that people who don't give much thought about the rights of others are the same ones who don't give much thought about their own rights of self-permission, self-trust, and self-love.

The whole point is that we can't have freedom for ourselves unless we respect the freedom of others. And we can't have freedom for ourselves unless we also accept the responsibly for doing what is necessary.

What I find amazing about people like this girl is that they are usually the first ones to complain when someone else does not follow the rules as they see them. The message that people like this young girl give is that they are special enough to break the rules, but no one else is.

Freedom not only means being responsible, it also means having the courage to do what is necessary and to accept the consequences of what you do.

When you make a choice you also need to accept the consequences of that choice. When you say something to another person you accept the possibility that person may not like what you say. When you enter into a race you accept the possibility that you may not win. When you make a friend you accept the possibility that your friend may not be a friend forever. When you try to do a job, you accept that you may fail.

Each time you act in a free way with responsibility, with courage, you make yourself stronger and you make it easier to make further free choices. When you show yourself that you can be trusted you make yourself more confident. You cannot be happy until you give yourself the permission and the freedom to be happy.

In the end, freedom is not something that is given to you. Freedom is something you learn, something you earn, a choice you make, a tool you can use.

Chapter 24

LOVE IS THE ULTIMATE I.Q. TEST

THE ELEPHANT EXPERTS

Six experts wanted to learn more about elephants. The problem was that they were blind and so were forced to use first hand information to satisfy their curiosity.

The first blind expert approached and happened to fall against the elephant's sturdy side.

"Amazing," he said, "an elephant is just like a wall."

The second approached from the front and his hands came upon the elephant's tusk.

"Amazing," said the second blind expert, "an elephant is round, and smooth and has a pointy end. An elephant is just like a spear."

The third expert reached out and happened to take the animal's trunk in his hands.

"Amazing," he said, "an elephant is a lot like a snake."

The fourth expert reached out and felt the animal's knee.

"Amazing," said the fourth, "an elephant is rough and round and sturdy and just like a tree."

The fifth expert happened to touch an ear.

"Amazing," the fifth said, "an elephant is a marvelous beast and is shaped just like a fan."

While groping with his hands the sixth blind expert happened to seize upon the elephant's swinging tail.

"Amazing," the expert said, "an elephant is very much like a rope."

And so the experts disputed, each holding his own opinion very strong, in spite of the fact that each was very wrong.

John G. Saxe

In one way or another all of us are as much elephant experts as those in Saxe's poem above. Somehow we have a great deal of difficulty identifying what is most important. We confuse the most visible things in life with the most important things in life, and as a result we often find that our days are full of walls, unpleasant fears, unrecognized feelings, unsolved problems and painful beliefs.

There really isn't anyone to blame for our confusion. Elephant experts tend to react most to what is most noticeable. This makes sense when survival means looking out for things which might be dangerous. But it doesn't make sense when we are trying to seek out the elements of life which we most need to understand in order to achieve some degree of personal effectiveness and happiness.

The chart below is only partial and while it would not be considered scientific, it nevertheless points to some important conclusions. It was assembled after reading the Saxe poem and wondering just what qualities the elephant experts had decided was significant about life. Because movies are a reflection of what we think is important and interesting, they also reflect our values, and so I turned to them for some answers.

Elephant Expert Visible & Important Checklist

Life Elements	Level Of Importance		
Visible In The Movies	Major	Mediocre	Minor
Power/Aggression	✓		
Wealth/Success	✓		
Guns/Violence	✓		
Fame/Fortune	✓		
Love			✓
Romance/Sex	✓		
Fancy Clothes		✓	
Motherhood			✓
Intelligence		✓	
Emotion/Feelings			✓
Anger/Fear	✓		

While these findings may be debatable, the direction they are pointing is not. With the help of our elephant experts we have decided that the things which are outside of us are more important than what is inside of us. We have evaluated, and we have decided that glitter is more important than content, that volume is more important than communication.

Teilhard de Chardin was a writer and thinker of some depth and perception. He spent a good deal of his life examining the findings of elephant experts and came to the conclusion that what we are looking for is not easily seen.

> The day will come when, after harnessing the winds, the tides, and gravitation, we shall harness the energies of love. And on that day, for the second time in the history of the world, humanity will have discovered fire.
>
> **Teilhard de Chardin**

There is no question that the discovery of fire changed the way we lived. Fire helped us keep our caves warm, helped us see in the dark, helped us cook our food, helped us stay cheerful on long winter nights, and in general helped us live longer, more fulfilling lives.

According to de Chardin, the discovery of love can do for us now what the discovery of fire did for us in our ancient history. In general, however, this has not yet happened. There is more passion and excitement given to buying a new washing machine, or a new set of tires for a bicycle, than there is in examining love or learning about its potential.

Fortunately we can make the leap from washing machines to love with ease. All we need to do is search for love and we will discover it in very personal ways. Love will come to us if we seek it, and when we do it will change everything that happens from then on - those are basic truths of the human universe.

When love comes it will change the way we see our friends and our enemies. It will change the way we understand our problems. It will change the meaning we attach to our feelings, and it will change how we evaluate our own sense of worth.

Love will make us stronger than we have ever been before.

We should be careful, however, that we don't repeat the mistakes made by the elephant experts. The most obvious definition of love will probably not be the most valuable definition. There are a lot of illusions out there in the world pretending to be something they are not, and this makes real love more difficult and more important than ever.

THE MODERN IMAGE OF LOVE

If you went up to a professional football player during the middle of a game and said that love is the most powerful energy in life, he would probably look at you as if you were crazy and point to the tons of beef and brawn on the field trying to destroy each other as proof that brute force is the most basic.

If you went to a law enforcement officer and said that love was more powerful than a gun, he or she might remind you that some criminals hurt other people because they like it, and love will not keep those outlaws behind bars or stop them from hurting other people in the future.

If you went to a school yard bully and said that love was more powerful than muscle there is little chance of agreement and a good chance of a bruise or two.

Most people do not connect the idea of love to something as forceful as power. Love is seen as something soft, mushy, maybe even a bit sissy, useful before marriage but not something to be prolonged, useful for mothers to help keep them feeling for their children, but not something to be taken seriously out of the family setting and into the real world.

The modern idea of love tries to reduce it to something that can be understood without a great deal of effort, and in this way makes it a little easier to control. Many times when we try to connect these duplicates back to the original knowledge of love we find that the connections are not so obvious.

Pretty girls, for example, in beer commercials sell a kind of love which can be bought by the case. How much this has to do with real love is not readily apparent. It is probably based upon love somehow, but the connection is thin at best.

Handsome guys with firm backsides shoved into tight jeans sell a kind of love which can be worn on the body rather than something which exists under the skin. How much this has to do with real love is not readily apparent. It is much easier to love a beer commercial or a pair of jeans than it is to love a real person, but at the same time it reduces the value of love to the point of meaninglessness.

Love is said to be what Valentine's Day and Cupid's arrows are all about, cute, sweet, and very easy. A good idea, perhaps, but without much depth or sincerity.

Many people believe that love can be conditional as in, "I will love you if..." This version of love suggests that it can be bought or sold or rented. Do this for me, and I will rent you some love. Stop doing this for me, and I will stop providing you with love.

WE DON'T STUDY WHAT WE CAN'T USE

Because love is difficult to pin down mathematically, we don't have a lot of computer programs trying to figure out what it is all about. True, a lot of microchip maidens are rescued in computer games, but this is more adventure than romance, and usually a lot of violence takes place before the maiden is free.

Because we can't kill a lot of people at once with it, love isn't analyzed in our chemistry labs and our universities. Hate, on the other hand, is widely studied in war colleges as an effective means of motivating soldiers to kill the current crop of bad guys. Love can't wage much destruction so it isn't taken as seriously as a club.

Real love is a non-profit way of thinking, so business isn't breaking down the gates to find out more about what it really means. The only real profit which seems to collect around love has to do with people feeling better inside, and because this can't be controlled or packaged it is generally disregarded.

Love won't help you pay the bill for new clothes or new shoes or a new bicycle, so it isn't a goal which is constantly on our minds.

REAL LOVE IS POWER

When we discover love we will find that it has everything to do with logic, clear thinking and strength, and very little to do with the lack of control which seems to be the modern idea of love as romance.

Love allows us to focus our thoughts and feelings so that we can cut through a lot of the unnecessary emotions and stumbling blocks which so easily seem to attach themselves to human relationships.

No one really knows what makes love happen, or just how important it is in the evolution of humanity, but that doesn't make it any less valuable to us personally. We don't have to know exactly what love is in order to be able to use it wisely.

We don't fall in love, we grow in love and into love. Love is something that develops inside our feelings and minds until gradually it becomes a directing force in our lives. The wonderful part about this growth is that as it becomes bigger inside of us, the world outside of us becomes bigger as well. This provides us with many more choices, possibilities, and options for success and enjoyment.

LOVE IS NOT A THING

Love is not a thing. It doesn't have a make and model. You can't say, "My love is a size 83. It has 10,000 square feet of space, three floors, 4 bedrooms and five bathrooms. It can go from 0 to 60 in 2.3 seconds, and it is so valuable I have to keep it in a vault in Switzerland."

Love is a feeling which allows you to look at people without being afraid of what they think, or what they say. The strength of this inner feeling can reach out and encompass others. You know they are separate beings, you know they might not even like you, yet the feeling you have understands that and doesn't get upset. That's real power.

When you love someone you can forgive them. This is a truly dynamic way to live because it refuses to allow you to hurt your own self for many of the silly and totally unnecessary things other people do or say to you.

Too often people treat us thoughtlessly, we feel bad as a result, and we carry that negative feeling with us for a long period of time. Meanwhile, the person who has hurt our feelings forgets what they have done to us. They may not even know they were hurting our feelings to begin with, so carrying the hurt they triggered inside of us makes the bad way we feel more painful.

It could possibly be that some of the people who hurt our feelings knew exactly what they were doing, and still did it to us deliberately. To carry that hurt inside us under those conditions is to give their hostility even more force, and in effect it allows them to control our lives.

It should always be remembered that other people do not really hurt our feelings or actually cause our feelings to be hurt. We give them that power to act in certain ways as triggers for us to feel bad in certain ways. And what we give them, we can also take away.

On a purely selfish level, the forgiveness of love helps us feel better. By not carrying around the hurt and bad feelings which others want to dump on us, we have more time to examine our own feelings and our own thoughts so that they can become more life-generating rather than destructive. Forgiveness makes us feel lighter because we give back the heaviness which other people want to transfer onto our shoulders through their own negativity.

Love allows us to trust ourselves. When we trust who we are we give ourselves permission to go beyond our limits, to break down walls and blow our fears away.

Giving ourselves permission to succeed is the first step along the way leading to success and allows us to recognize achievement when it comes. Permission allows us to accept failure when it comes, and not to make us feel inferior or unacceptable.

Trust in ourselves leads to trust in others. If I can trust in my own abilities to learn from failure, then I can also trust that others will also learn from their failures. And if they don't, then I can forgive them for not learning because ultimately they are living for reasons I do not, and will never be able to, understand.

People live the way they do, think, act and feel the way they do because they know facts only they can know as a result of living through experiences only they have endured - as a result they carry a history which only they can understand.

We are not always capable of relating a person's behavior back to their history, and in this way forgive them for how they behave toward us, nor is it our job to do so. Our job is to realize that many people are hurting badly inside, and as a result of their own pain the only way they know how to deal with life is to generate more pain and hurt.

There is nothing about love which says that you have to like people who are hurtful, difficult or deceitful, but it is definitely to your advantage to understand where they are coming from so that their ability to offend you collapses.

Love helps you understand and defuse criticism, condemnation and hostility. Hostile people have problems dealing with other people. When they criticize and disparage you they are not striking at you so much as they are striking at ghosts they carry with them and which just happen to fit their image of who you are. There have been a long line of people just like you who have been the target for their negativity, and there will be a long line after you.

Getting upset because of the attitude or remarks of others is as useless as yelling at the clock because it is telling you it is time to get out of bed.

People do not have to know you are special in order for you to feel that way. Love is always equal. Love helps you realize just how special you are, and if other people, for whatever reasons, can't understand your specialness, then you should not feel any less adequate.

At the same time, love helps you understand just how special other people are. Love helps you understand that hurting others really hurts you as much as it hurts them because it really acts to diminish your own specialness.

Love won't stop you from being mugged and it won't stop other people from trying to take advantage of you, but it will help you heal faster and it will help you maintain your own sense of well being.

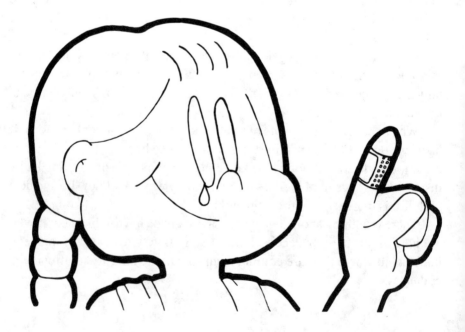

Love helps us understand that shame and guilt are not healthy nor are they necessary. Love helps us understand that all life is an experiment, and that guilt and shame are simply conclusions we reached in the past which we refuse to let go.

Love tells us to let go of bad feelings. Guilt is a bad feeling about something we did in the past. Worry is a bad feeling about what we will do in the future. Shame is a statement about how valueless we are. Love removes the emotional power from shame and worry and guilt and simply refuses to allow them to grow. Love lets you understand how unimportant these things really are.

Success is a basic part of love. Love won't help you get an 'A' grade on a test when you haven't studied for the test, nor will love get a report finished when you don't want to work on it. But love will help you heal the negative feelings you will get when you receive an 'E' instead of an 'A', and it will help you deal with the blast from your boss for your unfinished report.

LOVE IS HEALING

Healing is love and love is healing. That may sound like fuzzy thinking, but there is no other easy way to say it. Love brings healing just as surely as healing brings love because they are both different ways of saying the same thing.

Love heals mental and spiritual wounds in the same way that our immune system heals our cuts and scrapes and keeps us free from infection. The more our immune system loves the body it is protecting, the harder it will fight and the more vigilant it will be for unwanted sickness. An imbalanced mind weakens the body, and an unwell body weakens the mind. Good health, by itself, should be enough reason to convince us to choose love for our lives.

Love also helps healing by closing the gap between what we want and what we get, and in this way removing much of the stress and anxiety from our bodies so that they can concentrate on wellness and don't have to wear themselves out just trying to stay afloat.

Love promotes growth, and negativity stunts growth. Love stops pain and negativity magnifies pain and blows it all out of proportion.

TRY THIS EXPERIMENT

How do you usually react when you stub your toe? If you are like most people you will howl in pain, hobble around holding your aching toe, and sending shock waves of negative feelings and anger through your body and down to your toe. The angrier you are about the pain, the longer the pain continues, and the louder it gets in your body.

If you wish a perfect example of the difference between love and negative emotions, try this experiment.

The next time you stub your toe, deliberately stop yourself from getting excited, relax, lift your mind off the pain, and simply accept what is happening without getting angry. If you want to send love thoughts to help heal the soreness while you are defusing the ache that is even better.

Love neutralizes pain, and all other negative states because it helps us understand pain better. Either way, you will find that the pain will simply drop a level, ache for a minute or two in a dull way, and then simply fade away.

THE TECHNOLOGY OF LOVE

The human body and mind are not structured like a machine or a computer. In many ways this is too bad because there are times when it would be nice and convenient to have the ability to turn off our feelings or stop feeling depressed. Sometimes it might be nice just to turn everything off and do a Rip Van Winkle or a Science Officer Spock until all the negative stuff goes away.

Unfortunately, it is not possible to throw a mechanical switch or push a button to change the way we feel or to make our problems go away.

Drugs may seem like a simple switch, but they don't help us change the way we really feel, and they can't make our problems go away. Drugs only seem to help us feel better. They are an elephant expert's illusion.

Neither does alcohol change how we really feel. It only seems to make us feel different as if something is actually being done that will change us or help us over the long term.

In spite of the euphoric promise of both drugs and alcohol, the end result of relying on them for our well being is pain, emptiness, bitterness, wrongness, waste, and shortened lives.

Love, on the other hand, does make us feel better and it will continue to make us feel better for as long as we live. Love will change us. It will help us solve our problems in ways which will have lasting benefits.

But love will not come to us unless we actually make the effort to let it happen. We all have the power of love inside of us, but we do not all choose to take it up and make it our own.

We need to deliberately decide that we want love to fill us. We need to give love permission to operate our thoughts and our actions. When we give love permission to work for us, we begin an internal process which never fails to make us better people and enrich our lives.

It is true that we don't have mechanical buttons to change the mental programs we run or the way we function, but we do have biological equivalents to buttons, and we call them beliefs.

With a belief we can trigger a whole new way of thinking and a whole new way of acting. With a belief we can change the way we feel about things and we can change the way we understand life. Any belief we want can be constructed to start a change in the way ideas happen in our minds, to change the way feelings happen in our bodies, and to reshape the connections we have with other people.

The problem is that these biological buttons are not magical and effortless. They aren't as easy as turning on the television or dropping a pill or opening a bottle. They demand preparation, thoughtfulness, and persistence. They involve some planning and some effort. As soon as some people hear this they throw up their hands in despair and say they can't do it.

- I can't do it, it's too hard.
- There must be an easier way.
- Who needs love anyway.
- I can buy love.
- Who needs love, I have good looks.
- I don't want forgiveness, I want revenge.
- I exercise to keep my body in shape, who needs love?

Beliefs are the biological switches, and the factory process we use to build them is called learning. As we learn the importance of love, we not only build a belief we also construct a biological button which has the power to transform our lives.

When we turn on love with our beliefs we begin a self- reinforcing process which sends out positive energy into the world and receives positive energy from the world in return. The more positive energy which is received back, the stronger our ability to use love becomes, and this makes the whole process stronger.

In short form, here are the basic construction blocks of the biological belief switch for love. Make these blocks your own, and you will turn on love in your life.

BIOLOGICAL BELIEF SWITCH FOR LOVE

- Love is stronger than hate
- Love requires effort
- Love is not in short supply
- Love is not sissy or easy
- Love makes us feel better
- Love helps us solve problems
- Love is a way of life
- Love is not something you can buy
- Love is more than tight jeans and a good body
- Love is more than money
- Love helps us stay healthy
- Love helps us forgive
- Love helps us trust ourselves
- Love defuses the efforts of difficult people
- Love is hard work at the beginning
- Love is not competitive
- Love is not selfish
- Love can protect our feelings

It is highly unlikely that elephant experts would agree that love is as powerful as outlined here. Naked aggression just seems to be so much stronger in comparison to love that any contest between the two would appear to be totally unequal.

But when we examine aggression we find that aggression breeds aggression in return. Examining hate we find that hate breeds hate. Force breeds force. Coercion breeds coercion. Not only do these negative motivations cause an equal an opposite backlash, they are only effective in the short term. Remove the force, the coercion, the aggression, and immediately everything that was suppressed snaps back to the way it was before the influence was used.

So what exactly does aggression do for us? Just how is it more powerful than love when it causes a powerful backlash?

You can force a person to bend to your will, and that may be an example of the influence of negative force in action, but that person may spend a lifetime trying to get back at you. Or the anger that results may be aimed at you for years to come. So what have you won?

Love, on the other hand, begets love. Give love out, and love comes back. Not from everyone, but from enough sources to make you larger and stronger and more certain of yourself. Add this to the electrifying and sensational feeling that love gives you, and what this amounts to is an extremely effective, intelligent, and focused way of life.

LOVE IS THE ULTIMATE I.Q. TEST

> For one human being to love another:
> that is perhaps the most difficult
> of all tasks, the ultimate,
> the last test and proof, the work
> for which all other work
> is but preparation.
>
> **Rainer Maria Rilke**

You will pass and fail tests all your life. Sometimes you won't even know that you are involved in a test. From start to finish, life is one challenge after another, one surprise after another, one test after another.

If you flunk a subject at school you always have the option of taking it over again. As far we know, if you flunk life there is no chance of taking it over again. There is no summer school or night school. It is now or never.

There is no scientific or mathematical way of judging how well we are living. Life is too big to be analyzed that way. But if we look at love as the most positive expression of life, then it is possible to test how well we are doing in life simply by calculating how much love exists in the life we are leading.

Love is a way of living that is entirely different than any other way of living. People aren't going to come up to you and say, "Oh, what a loving life you are leading." A loving life is not always visible from the outside. But love is visible on the inside.

You will know if you are leading a loving life because the quality of your feelings, your actions, your thinking and what you know about the world will be stimulating and enlightening. When you feel this way, you will have passed the ultimate I.Q. test .

With love as your internal consultant you will have an increased ability to meet your problems in ways which will bring self respect not only for yourself but also for others.

Let love become your automatic pilot and you will find your drive through life to be a stimulating, fascinating adventure. You will meet challenges with confidence and deal with surprises with effectiveness.

Let love tell you how fast to go and when to put on the breaks. This will reduce stress and anxiety and impatience.

Let love define what to value and what not to value. This will increase the extent of your limits and remove a great deal of uncertainty.

Let love help you set your goals and evaluate your progress. This will keep you encouraged and enthusiastic. You will want to persist because you will know with confidence that no matter what happens you will succeed.

Let love help you relate to other people, and to life in general, and you will have provided your motivational engine with a virtual guarantee for success, happiness, contentment, and effectiveness.

Life is simple in a complicated way. Your choices make the difference, that is the simple part, and you have millions of choices from which to choose, that is the complicated part. Let love help you make your decisions and you will experience results which will make you proud, and fill you with a power which cannot be deflated or destroyed.

A PLAN
FOR STEERING YOURSELF
IN THE RIGHT
DIRECTION

FIND YOUR BELIEF QUOTIENT

Your motivation is the engine which drives you. It shapes the way you act, the way you feel, and what you think. It determines your conduct, your degree of self-control, and your self-confidence.

Motivation even determines the way you study and how well you learn.

Motivation is made up of beliefs. How well your motivation works for you is determined by how well all your beliefs work together.

The following Belief Test is based upon the ideas outlined in MOTIVATING CHILDREN. Your final score will give you an idea how well your beliefs are working for you.

Read each belief listed below carefully . If you agree with the statement, circle YES; if you aren't certain, circle MAYBE; and if you disagree, circle NO.

At the end of each page add up the total number of YESs, MAYBEs and NOs. At the end of the test add the total number of each in their columns .

The analysis after the test will provide you with your Belief Quotient .

BELIEF INVENTORY

1. You get from life only what you put into life.   YES   MAYBE   NO

2. Success can only be achieved with hard work and a great deal of effort.   YES   MAYBE   NO

3. Other people can help you, but what you make of yourself is entirely up to you.   YES   MAYBE   NO

4. You are a very special person with a right to self-confidence, success, and happiness.   YES   MAYBE   NO

Total _____

5. Other people may have more power, more money, more success and may even be nicer looking, but that does not mean they are any better than you.　　YES　MAYBE　NO

6. Your beliefs are responsible for the motivation which controls your life.　　YES　MAYBE　NO

7. You can gain some control over what motivates you simply by changing your beliefs.　　YES　MAYBE　NO

8. Problems don't go away just because we want them to.　　YES　MAYBE　NO

9. Real intelligence means that you accept responsibility for your actions and for the results of those actions.　　YES　MAYBE　NO

10. Wishing for luck is not the same thing as taking action to make luck happen for you.　　YES　MAYBE　NO

11. A major portion of the luck which comes to you is a direct result of the actions you take.　　YES　MAYBE　NO

12. Who you are now is the result of all the choices you have made in the past.　　YES　MAYBE　NO

13. If you want to take a good look at who you are, all you need to do is look at the kinds of choices you make each day.　　YES　MAYBE　NO

14. The more we are afraid of our feelings the harder they are to control.　　YES　MAYBE　NO

15. Our feelings provide us with information without words about what is happening around us, and inside of us.　　YES　MAYBE　NO

16. Smiling can help us change the way we feel and this can make the world a better place in which to live.　　YES　MAYBE　NO

17. It takes a lot of work not to feel defeated simply because it seems that you are.　　YES　MAYBE　NO

Total _____

18. We are not always responsible for the urges   YES   MAYBE   NO
and thoughts which come to us.

19. We are responsible for the thoughts which   YES   MAYBE   NO
stay around and which we act upon.

20. Success in something does not guarantee   YES   MAYBE   NO
that life will become better for you.

21. Positive thoughts create a different world   YES   MAYBE   NO
from the one created by negative thoughts.

22. Feeling bad can become the only way of life   YES   MAYBE   NO
you know.

23. Knowing what is right does not always help   YES   MAYBE   NO
us do what is right.

24. We can change our beliefs by changing the   YES   MAYBE   NO
way we think, the way we act, the things we
know, and the feelings we have.

25. By changing the solutions to our problems   YES   MAYBE   NO
we can change the kind of problems which will
come next.

26. Life is made up of a long series of problems   YES   MAYBE   NO
which are connected by the solutions we
choose.

27. The quality of our solutions determines the   YES   MAYBE   NO
quality of our lives.

28. The fears we have determine the choices we   YES   MAYBE   NO
make and the goals we set.

29. Fear create more fears.   YES   MAYBE   NO

30. Fears are difficult to overcome, but with   YES   MAYBE   NO
practice and persistence they can be mastered.

31. Big fears act like walls to prevent us from   YES   MAYBE   NO
doing some things we might enjoy.

Total _____

32. Mental walls keep us safe, but they also stop us from changing and improving ourselves.　　　YES　　MAYBE　　NO

33. By giving yourself permission to fail you also give yourself permission to succeed.　　　YES　　MAYBE　　NO

34. Anger is normal, but that doesn't make it right.　　　YES　　MAYBE　　NO

35.. The things which happened to you in the past will only bother you if you let it.　　　YES　　MAYBE　　NO

36. Continuous anger can damage your health.　　　YES　　MAYBE　　NO

37. We don't need proof of any kind to believe something is true - all we really need is to want to believe it is true.　　　YES　　MAYBE　　NO

38. You generally KAN'T do what you believe you KAN'T do.　　　YES　　MAYBE　　NO

39. Conforming often makes life easier for us, but that doesn't mean that it makes life better.　　　YES　　MAYBE　　NO

40. Your motivation can be imagined as your automatic pilot driving you down the highway.　　　YES　　MAYBE　　NO

41. Your automatic pilot knows where to steer and what to do by the beliefs and habits which you have learned.　　　YES　　MAYBE　　NO

42. To change how our automatic pilot works all we have to do is change our beliefs.　　　YES　　MAYBE　　NO

43. Failure is not a statement about who we are.　　　YES　　MAYBE　　NO

44. We can learn from failure because it tells us what works and what doesn't work.　　　YES　　MAYBE　　NO

45. If you can't find love, then you are looking in the wrong places, and if you can't hold onto it then you aren't holding the real thing.　　　YES　　MAYBE　　NO

Total _____

46. The way we talk in our heads can help us   YES   MAYBE   NO
solve problems, motivate ourselves, and make
us feel happy.

47. The way we talk in our heads can make us   YES   MAYBE   NO
feel miserable, depressed, and unsuccessful.

48. If you want to feel guilty and depressed,   YES   MAYBE   NO
then don't get plenty of exercise, eat the right
foods, and get the right amount of sleep.

49. Freedom not only means being responsible,   YES   MAYBE   NO
it also means having the courage to accept the
consequences of what you do.

50. Love is an exceptionally powerful force we   YES   MAYBE   NO
can use to make ourselves feel stronger.

Total _____

HOW TO CALCULATE YOUR BELIEF QUOTIENT

To determine your Belief Quotient, add the NOs, the MAYBEs and the YESs. Give one point for each YES, and a half point (1/2) for each MAYBE. A NO response does not receive a mark.

NOs _____ MAYBEs _____ YESs _____ TOTAL

Marks _____   _____   _____   _____

Find your score in the set of marks in the column under the Belief Score on the next page.

Now, move horizontally across the page to find the matching number under the Belief Quotient column.

Your Belief Quotient will give you a mathematical idea about how well you are using the beliefs discussed in this book. This information should then help you decide the steps to take to fine tune your motivation engine.

A high B.Q. means that you are using your beliefs in a positive, life-enhancing way. Your motivation is driving you forward effectively and you have a clear grasp of what you can do to be happy, successful and self-fulfilled.

BELIEF SCALE

Belief Score	Belief Quotient
50-46	10
45-40	9
39-35	8
34-30	7
29-25	6
24-20	5
19-15	4
14-10	3
9-5	2
4-0	1

A low B.Q. means yor beliefs are sometimes working against each other. Your motivation is not as clearly defined as it could be. You will find that your thinking does not always match your feelings, and your actions are not always what you want.

Your B.Q. is not fixed. A low B.Q. now does not doom you to a low B.Q. score in the future. Our responses will not always be the same because we will be different people tomorrow than we are today and as a result we will make different choices.

MOTIVATING CHILDREN has been written to help you understand that the choices you make are a result of the beliefs which make up your motivation engine. If you do not like the way things are going for you now, then you cannot expect people or events to do the changing. Only you can do the changing.

You cannot control life, or what happens to you, but you can change the way you react to what happens, and in that way you change life.

A PLAN
FOR STEERING YOURSELF
IN THE RIGHT
DIRECTION

Why not drop me a line?

I hope you enjoyed reading this book, and I also hope you found the information useful.

Listed below are a number of good reasons why you might want to contact me:

☑ You are a child with a problem and you want to write to someone who will listen

☑ You have any thoughts, experiences or anecdotes you would like to share

☑ You wish more information concerning seminars and workshops on PARENTING, MOTIVATION, PROBLEM SOLVING, SELF-ESTEEM, and BELIEF TECHNOLOGY

☑ You wish to clarify something I said.

☑ You just feel like writing a letter.

Please forward all correspondence to:

> Gordon Nosworthy
> c/o Learning Path Publications
> Box 273
> Thornhill, Ontario
> Canada
> L3T 3N3

MOTIVATING CHILDREN WORKBOOK

The MOTIVATING CHILDREN WORKBOOK is full of ideas for extending beliefs and developing a healthy, functioning motivation system. The material has been designed to be entertaining as well as informative. The games and exercises can be completed by a child alone or in company with an adult.

Learning Path Publications		ORDER FORM
MOTIVATING CHILDREN	$12.95	$3.00
MOTIVATING CHILDREN WORKBOOK	$ 7.95	$3.00
MOTIVATING CHILDREN + WORKBOOK	$20.00	$4.00

NOTE: WORKBOOK will be available in December 1992.

Send check or money order for $_____ Payable to Learning Path Publications. Allow 2 weeks for delivery.

Send to:
Name _____
Address _____
City _____ Province _____
Postal Code _____ Phone _____

❑ **Yes, I am interested in receiving information about seminars.**
❑ **Yes, I am interested in organizing a seminar for a School, an Organization, or a Parent Group.**